WARRIORS

CODE OF THE CLANS

EXPLORE THE WARRIORS WORLD

WARRIORS

Book One: Into the Wild

Book Two: Fire and Ice

Book Three: Forest of Secrets

Book Four: Rising Storm

Book Five: A Dangerous Path

Book Six: The Darkest Hour

THE NEW PROPHECY

Book One: Midnight

Book Two: Moonrise

Book Three: Dawn

Book Four: Starlight

Book Five: Twilight

Book Six: Sunset

POWER OF THREE

Book One: The Sight

Book Two: Dark River

Book Three: Outcast

Book Four: Eclipse

Book Five: Long Shadows

Book Six: Sunrise

MANGA

The Lost Warrior

Warrior's Refuge

Warrior's Return

The Rise of Scourge

Tigerstar and Sasha #1: Into the Woods

Tigerstar and Sasha #2: Escape from the Forest

Tigerstar and Sasha #3: Return to the Clans

SPECIALS

Warriors Field Guide: Secrets of the Clans

Warriors Super Edition: Firestar's Quest

Warriors: Cats of the Clans

Also by Erin Hunter
SEEKERS

Book One: The Quest Begins

Book Two: Great Bear Lake

Book Three: Smoke Mountain

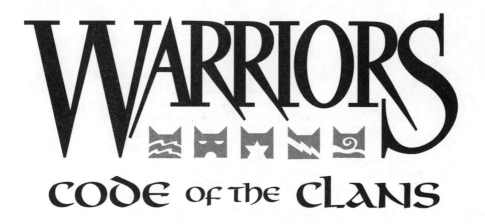

WARRIORS

CODE OF THE CLANS

ERIN HUNTER

ILLUSTRATED BY WAYNE McLOUGHLIN

HarperCollins*Publishers*

Library of Congress Cataloging-in-Publication Data

Hunter, Erin.

Code of the Clans / Erin Hunter ; illustrated by Wayne McLoughlin.—1st ed.

p. cm.—(Warriors)

Summary: Explores the fifteen rules that govern the daily life of a warrior cat.

ISBN 978-0-06-166009-2 (trade bdg.)—ISBN 978-0-06-166010-8 (lib. bdg.)

[1. Cats—Fiction. 2. Fantasy.] I. McLoughlin, Wayne, ill. II. Title.

PZ7.H916625Co 2009   2008045061

[Fic]—dc22

Typography by Larissa Lawrynenko

09 10 11 12 13 LP/WOR 10 9 8 7 6 5 4 3 2

❖

First Edition

For Mr. Pugh, with love

Special thanks to Victoria Holmes

CONTENTS

WARRIORS

CODE of the CLANS

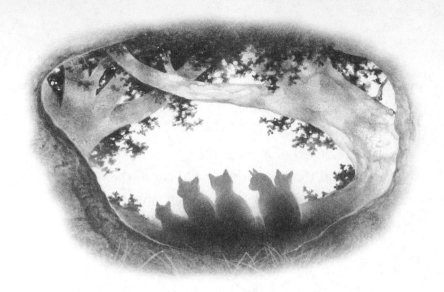

THE DAWN
OF THE CLANS

Many moons ago, a community of cats settled in dense woodland close to the edge of a moor. Some were kittypets intrigued by the idea of exploring beyond their housefolk's backyard; others had been born and raised in the wild, by cats who knew how to catch their own prey and find shelter in the cold nights of leaf-bare.

The woodland, with the river running fast and deep at the edge of the trees, proved to be good territory for the cats. There was enough shelter for every cat, enough prey to feed them all, and the freedom to hunt among the trees, on the open moor, and along the fish-filled river.

The cats began to settle according to their preferences for hunting and prey. The fish-eaters kept mostly to the banks of the river, making their dens among the reeds and twisted willow roots; the mouse-pouncers stayed under the densest trees, perfecting their leaps among the tangled undergrowth; the rabbit-chasers, faster and leaner than the other cats, kept to the open moor; the squirrel-stalkers settled in the sparser woodland, where they learned to climb trees and hunt among the branches; and the cats who had a taste for snakes and lizards, and the cunning to catch them on marshy ground, settled among brittle grass stalks and rattling pine trees on the farthest edge of the territory.

There were no borders at first, and within each hunting ground the cats lived separately, meeting only as they went in pursuit of the same prey. Occasionally cats clashed over a piece of fresh-kill or a good place for a den, but battles between large numbers of cats were unheard of.

Then a time came when prey was scarce, and there were too many mouths to feed and bodies to shelter in each hunting ground. Battles broke out, just a few cats at first, but more and more until hunting ground took on hunting ground, fighting for survival, not just for themselves, but for the cats who lived alongside them. After one dreadful battle, when the ground beneath the four great oak trees turned red with blood, the spirits of the dead cats came back to plead for peace with the strongest cats from each hunting ground: Wind, River, Thunder, Shadow, and Sky.

The five vowed to their fallen companions that they would find a way to put an end to the fighting, to live in their separate hunting grounds in communities that would preserve each territory for generations of cats to come.

THE TIME OF THE CLANS HAD BEGUN...

THE WARRIOR CODE

1. Defend your Clan, even with your life. You may have friendships with cats from other Clans, but your loyalty must remain to your Clan.

2. Do not hunt or trespass on another Clan's territory.

3. Elders and kits must be fed before apprentices and warriors.

4. Prey is killed only to be eaten. Give thanks to StarClan for its life.

5. A kit must be at least six moons old to become an apprentice.

6. Newly appointed warriors will keep a silent vigil for one night after receiving their warrior name.

7. A cat cannot be made deputy without having mentored at least one apprentice.

8. The deputy will become Clan leader when the leader dies or retires.

9. After the death or retirement of the deputy, the new deputy must be chosen before moonhigh.

10. A gathering of all Clans is held at the full moon during a truce that lasts for the night. There shall be no fighting among Clans at this time.

11. Boundaries must be checked and marked daily. Challenge all trespassing cats.

12. No warrior may neglect a kit in pain or in danger, even if that kit is from a different Clan.

13. The word of the Clan leader is the warrior code.

14. An honorable warrior does not need to kill other cats to win his or her battles, unless they are outside the warrior code or it is necessary for self-defense.

15. A warrior rejects the soft life of a kittypet.

WELCOME TO THE WARRIOR CODE

hello! Firestar told me you'd be visiting today. Come in. Watch out for the brambles at the entrance; they've grown faster than ever with the warm rain we've had this moon. Sorry, did that one catch on your pelt? I have some marigold leaves if it's cut you. No? Good. My name is Leafpool, by the way, and I'm ThunderClan's medicine cat—but I expect you knew that, didn't you? I forget how well-known our Clan has become, even among loners and kittypets.

Sit down, please, and make yourself comfortable. We have a lot to talk about!

Firestar said that you wanted to learn about the warrior code. I can see how it would fascinate you, born and raised outside the Clans. Does it seem as if our lives are governed by strict, ancient rules? Your life must feel free as air in comparison; you can hunt when you like, eat what you catch, and choose friends and enemies wherever you please without having loyalties and responsibilities forced upon you. I can see by the glint in your eyes that you sometimes pity us for the code that binds us like bramble tendrils to our Clanmates, our territories, and our long-dead ancestors. But the warrior code isn't like that. If you're born to it, raised in its nurturing paws, it feels as obvious as breathing.

You hunt just for yourself, yes? But what would happen if you got injured or sick? In the Clans, the strongest cats, the warriors, hunt for all of us. And when it is their turn to have graying muzzles and trembling paws, new warriors will catch prey for them until they walk with StarClan and hunt like young cats once more.

You think the Clans hate one another and fight all the time. It's true, we live in close quarters with the other Clans, and that can lead to tension, but we also unite against common enemies— you heard about the badger attack, yes? We would have been destroyed if WindClan hadn't come to help us. And when we had to leave the forest, four Clans succeeded in making the Great Journey where one alone would have starved or frozen to death.

Being part of a Clan means knowing that you'll never be alone. The life of the Clan surrounds you and stretches into the distance as far as your imagination can see. You follow in the paw steps of Clanmates born moons before you and those who are younger will follow your paw steps in moons to come. You will always be part of your Clan, even when you walk among your ancestors in the stars.

You're still uncertain, aren't you? No matter. Wait until you hear how each part of the code came about. No, I am not going to tell you stories. Relax your mind and together we will travel back through the ages, through many generations of cats. Just as grass grows even on the bare cliffs around the hollow, each code arose from the Clans' daily lives as a way of ensuring that every cat was safe, nurtured, and fed from its very first breath. You will see that while the warrior code is still a force for good, for protection and balance among the Clans, many cats have challenged it—for it can bring terrible conflict to individual lives.

Are you ready? Let us begin with the first code. . . .

�

CODE ONE

It's hard to imagine a time when cats were allowed to have friendships with cats in other Clans. I know better than most cats the agony of loving a cat from a different Clan— and of knowing that I had to return to my own Clanmates because they needed me, and because I wanted to remain loyal to the warrior code. Come with me, and let me show you the sad fate of Ryewhisker and Cloudberry. Though it breaks my heart, you will see why this terrible piece of the code came to be. As every cat must learn, the strength of the entire Clan depends on the loyalty of each one of its members.

The Beginning of the Warrior Code

"**R**ace you to the hawthorn bush!"

"Not fair, Ryewhisker! You know you'll win!" protested Cloudberry.

Ryewhisker turned to look back at the dark gray she-cat. Cloudberry was slender for a RiverClan cat, but her fur was thick and sleek.

"I'll give you a head start," he offered. Cloudberry tipped her head on one side, her blue eyes sparkling. "Or . . . or I'll close my eyes, or run backward, or carry a stone in my mouth. . . ."

"Bee-brain," she purred. She padded up to him and rubbed her head against his cheek. "I'll race you to the hawthorn if you race me across the river."

Ryewhisker backed away, shaking his head. "No way! You can't tell me it's natural to get your fur wet! I tried it once, don't you remember?"

"You fell off a stepping-stone! Hardly a proper way to start swimming!"

Ryewhisker reached out with his tail to touch Cloudberry's flank. "Do you think our kits will be able to run fast and swim?" he meowed softly.

Cloudberry stared at him in astonishment. "How did you know? I . . . I was going to tell you, I promise, but I wasn't sure how you'd feel. I thought you might want WindClan kits. . . ."

Ryewhisker let out a frustrated *mrrrow*. "They will be WindClan kits! And RiverClan kits! They will be ours, and that's all that matters! Do your Clanmates know?"

The she-cat began to roll some small stones restlessly beneath

her paw. "Not yet. I wanted to tell you first."

"You're worried about what your father will say, aren't you?" Ryewhisker guessed.

Cloudberry looked up at him, her eyes pleading. "Emberstar is a good leader. You can't blame him for wanting more RiverClan kits. We need more warriors after that bout of greencough in leaf-bare."

"But they *will* be RiverClan kits!" Ryewhisker reminded her. He flicked his tail impatiently. "I'll let you teach them to swim as soon as they open their eyes!"

"Then you'll let me raise them in RiverClan?" Cloudberry queried.

Ryewhisker blinked. He hadn't thought that far ahead. "Well, yes," he meowed. "I'll come stay with you when they're born, of course. Your father has never minded me staying in your camp. And you can bring them to WindClan when they're old enough to walk that far."

Cloudberry nodded, but her eyes were still troubled. Ryewhisker pressed his muzzle against her ear. "It'll be fine," he promised. "Every cat knows that Emberstar's closest friend is Thistletail, in ThunderClan. If any cat understands that friendships don't stop at the border of a territory, it's Emberstar."

"But what about the stolen fish?" Cloudberry asked. Last moon, RiverClan had accused WindClan of stealing fish from the river and had sent a patrol to Duststar, WindClan's leader, to warn him to keep away. Duststar had insisted his Clan would never eat fish, but Ryewhisker knew the RiverClan cats were still suspicious.

"We didn't take those fish," he told Cloudberry. "Maybe these kits will bring our Clans together again."

Cloudberry relaxed against him and Ryewhisker closed his eyes, imagining tiny lives stirring within her, dark gray like their mother or brown tabby like him, swift-pawed and strong swimmers. These kits would bring peace between the two Clans, he was sure of it.

"WindClan! Retreat!"

Ryewhisker shook his head to clear the blood from his eyes as Stonetail yowled the order. The big gray tom was standing on a tree stump, wild-eyed as he called to his Clanmates to leave the battleground. Ryewhisker leaped back, freeing the RiverClan warrior from beneath his paws. This fight was all RiverClan's fault! They had accused WindClan twice more of stealing fish and threatened to tell the other Clans that the cats on the moor were thieves and trespassers. As if any WindClan warriors would get their paws wet chasing that slimy prey! Duststar had decided that the only way to stop the complaints was to teach RiverClan that WindClan cats were strong enough to catch their own prey—and well-enough fed not to need anyone else's.

"Retreat!" Stonetail yowled again.

"Mouse-hearted cowards!" spat a

RiverClan warrior behind them.

"If you're going to steal our fish, you should make sure you're strong enough to fight us for it!" hissed another.

Ryewhisker felt the fur stand up along his spine, and his paws tingled with the urge to spin around and claw their ears. When would these dumb cats realize that WindClan was not stealing their precious fish? The reeds closed around them as they headed back toward the Twoleg bridge, and for a moment Ryewhisker could hear nothing except his Clanmates' panting and the rattling of the brittle stalks.

"Stop right there!" screeched a voice up ahead.

Ryewhisker collided with Hawkfur's haunches as the black warrior halted in front of him. Peering past his Clanmate, he saw a ginger-and-white RiverClan warrior glaring at Stonetail, blocking his way.

"You didn't think we'd let you go so easily, did you?" growled the RiverClan cat.

Stonetail didn't flinch. "We'll continue to fight if we have to," he replied. "Is that what you want?"

The RiverClan warrior bared his teeth. "This fight is far from over!" He sprang at Stonetail, who rolled onto his back, scrabbling at his attacker's belly with his hind paws. The reeds clattered together and more RiverClan warriors rushed forward, leaping onto the WindClan cats. A stocky gray tabby sank its claws into Ryewhisker's shoulder and dragged him onto the ground. Ryewhisker ripped himself free, blood soaking into his fur, and jumped at the warrior with all four paws stretched out. The warrior crouched low and sprang up to meet him, knocking him out of the air and grappling with him as they fell side by side, lying half in and half out of the reeds.

Ryewhisker found himself being smothered by thick gray fur.

He wrenched his head up to draw breath—and stared straight into the startled blue eyes of Cloudberry. As he watched, a dark shadow reared up behind her, claws glinting in the sun, and plunged down onto her neck.

"No!" screeched Ryewhisker, leaping up so violently that the attacker, Ryewhisker's Clanmate Hawkfur, tumbled off into the reeds.

"Ryewhisker, you can't do this!" called the gray she-cat, who was struggling to her paws. "We have to fight our own battles!"

Ryewhisker glanced at her over his shoulder. "You think I'm going to let our kits be harmed by my own Clanmate?"

Hawkfur stared at him in disbelief. "Kits?" he echoed.

The brown tabby met his gaze. "Cloudberry is expecting my kits. I cannot let you hurt her."

"Look out!" screeched Cloudberry.

There was a thunder of paws, abruptly cut off as a broad-shouldered RiverClan warrior leaped into the air. Then a soft thud as Ryewhisker's legs folded under the weight of his attacker and he slumped to the ground, his eyes already closed. Blood pooled out from his shoulder, dark and shiny on the wet ground. The gray tabby scrambled off him, shaking his pelt.

Cloudberry didn't move, just stared at the limp brown body. "Oh, Ryewhisker, what have you done?" she whispered.

"Is every Clan here?" Duststar called from on top of the huge gray rock. All around him, trees murmured softly in the night breeze, casting blurred shadows across the moonlit hollow. Duststar had asked the other leaders to meet him here because the hollow lay at the center of the Clans, yet it belonged to none since the battle that had separated the Clans for the very first time. The elders who could recall that battle stayed away from the hollow, convinced that the bloodstains would never be washed out of the grass. Duststar had chosen the night of the full moon because it would enable cats to travel safely—and offer none the temptation of darkness to launch an unsuspected attack.

"We are here," replied Birchstar, leader of SkyClan. He sprang onto the rock to join Duststar, his strong haunches powering him up. The other leaders, unwilling to be left at the foot of the rock, scrambled up, too: Emberstar from RiverClan, Hollystar from ShadowClan, and Whitestar from ThunderClan, whose pelt glowed as bright as the moon in the half-light. The rest of the cats stayed on the ground, a patrol from each Clan, gazing somberly up at the leaders with their tails tucked over their paws.

"If you're going to blame my Clan for the death of your warrior—" Emberstar began, raising his hackles.

Duststar shook his head. "No, Emberstar, that's not why I asked you all to come here. Ryewhisker's death is a tragedy we can ill afford after such a hard leaf-bare, but it would not have happened if he had not been . . . attached . . . to Cloudberry." He looked down at the RiverClan cats, but Cloudberry was not among them. She was probably too close to having her kits.

"From now on, cats must be loyal only to their own Clanmates. Friendships with cats from another territory must be put aside for the sake of their Clan. We cannot allow our warriors to be distracted in battle or to fight for anything other than what is best for their own Clan. Are we agreed?"

Whitestar stood up. "Clan above all else. It makes sense to me."

Hollystar and Birchstar nodded. Emberstar meowed, "Well said, Duststar. My Clan is sorry for the loss of your warrior. But from now on, each Clan stands—and fights—alone."

"If we have less contact across borders, how will we let one another know about something that could be important, such as the arrival of foxes or Twoleg interference?" asked Hollystar, her blue eyes like tiny pieces of sky.

"We could meet here every full moon, when the forest is light enough to walk easily, and come in peace to share our news," Birchstar suggested.

"A truce?" Duststar meowed.

There was a shocked murmuring among the cats of all Clans.

"We cannot promise peace when ThunderClan steals our prey!" hissed an elderly WindClan warrior.

"And we cannot promise peace while WindClan attacks our border patrols!" meowed a ThunderClan warrior with a torn ear.

"And which of the Clans can trust ShadowClan?" asked another cat.

A great yowling broke out among all the cats.

"Enough!" Duststar growled. He stretched to his full height and stared down at the cats in the hollow. "Birchstar, I see more clearly than ever that your suggestion is wise. Though I doubt any peace will hold even for one night, let us try it and see what it brings."

"That's all I ask," Birchstar meowed.

"Cats of all the Clans!" Duststar continued. "From now on you must defend your Clan, even with your life. You may have friendships with cats from other Clans, but your loyalty must remain to your Clan, as one day you may meet cats you have befriended in battle. This will be our code, the law of warriors, and it is up to each one of us to carry it in our hearts. Until the next full moon, may StarClan guide your path."

He jumped down from the rock and, with a flick of his tail, led the WindClan cats out of the hollow, toward the moon-washed moor.

CODE TWO

**DO NOT HUNT OR TRESPASS
ON ANOTHER CLAN'S TERRITORY.**

*We take it for granted now that each Clan lives in the
territory best suited to provide food for its particular hunting skills.
But come with me to the time before borders were fixed, when
cats took food from other territories if their own ran short. You will
see that this code was needed, because if anything
is likely to cause trouble, it's theft of precious fresh-kill.*

Finders Keepers

Three seasons had passed since the leaders of the Clans decided to meet in peace each full moon, and the truce had held. Stonestar, the WindClan leader, stood on the Great Rock and surveyed the cats filing into the moonlit hollow. Their pelts stood out sharply against the snow, apart from Whitestar of ThunderClan, who was only visible when he looked up and Stonestar caught a glimpse of his dark eyes.

Whitestar, Emberstar, Birchstar, and Brindlestar, the new leader of ShadowClan, joined him on the rock. The leaders nodded to one another before standing in a line to look down on the cats below.

As the oldest leader, Emberstar was usually the first to speak, but Brindlestar didn't give him a chance. "I have a complaint against ThunderClan!" she declared.

Whitestar faced her, his tail twitching. "We aren't the ones stealing prey!" he hissed. "You can't complain because our patrols drive you out every time."

"It's not stealing!" Brindlestar snapped. "What are we meant to eat, if we can't find prey in our own territory?"

"Each Clan lives in the place where it is best suited to hunting," Birchstar pointed out.

"Yeah, since when did ShadowClan start hunting in undergrowth and through brambles?" challenged Vinetail, ThunderClan's deputy.

"Since we started starving in our own territory," growled Lakestorm, the ShadowClan deputy.

Stonestar stepped forward. "ShadowClan should keep to its own prey," he meowed firmly. "No Clan has prey to spare, especially not during leaf-bare."

"Then what are we supposed to eat?" yowled Lakestorm. His voice cut through the icy air, and for a moment the hollow fell silent. Then a creaking sound began. . . .

Stonestar peered up, trying to see where the noise was coming from. In the clearing, the cats huddled together in their Clans, too scared to flee.

Crashhhhhh!

A huge branch ripped away from one of the giant oaks and plunged onto the cats, sending flurries of snowflakes into the air. Stonestar watched in horror as the cats vanished in a swirling cloud of snow and twigs.

"SkyClan! SkyClan! Is every cat all right?" Birchstar ran to the edge of the rock and peered down, calling to her Clanmates.

CODE THREE

Whitestar and Brindlestar joined her, yowling into the cloud.

"Wait!" Whitestar ordered. Pushing his way through the other leaders, he turned to face them. "One at a time, or no cat will hear you. Birchstar, you go first." He stepped back, and only his trembling paws showed how terrified he was for the safety of his own Clan.

"SkyClan cats! Can you hear me?" Birchstar yowled.

There was a muffled sound, then a speckled gray head popped up at the edge of the hollow. It was Rainsplash, the deputy. "We're all here, Birchstar!" he called.

Stonestar stepped forward. The ground seemed a long way down, a mess of churned snow divided by a huge black branch bristling with twigs. "WindClan? Are you there?"

Mudpuddle, the brown-and-white deputy, scrambled up from the far side of the clearing. "All safe, Stonestar!" he reported, and Stonestar let out his breath in relief.

Emberstar quickly established that the RiverClan cats had been too far back to be hit by the falling branch. That left ThunderClan and ShadowClan. The branch had toppled right into the center of the Gathering, directly onto the two quarreling Clans.

Brindlestar walked to the edge of the rock. "ShadowClan, are you all right?"

The leaders waited in silence. Heartbeats passed, broken only by the faint plop of snow sliding from the trees. Then, "We're all okay, Brindlestar!" A bundle of twigs rattled together at one side of the branch, and Lakestorm pushed his way out. Once he was free, he turned to help his Clanmates out behind him.

Brindlestar narrowed her eyes, checking each member of her patrol. She nodded. "Lakestorm's right," she murmured. "ShadowClan is safe."

Now it was Whitestar's turn. Stonestar held his breath again. There was no way that branch could have fallen into the hollow without crushing several cats. It was too big, too heavy. It had carved too great a slice through the clearing. . . .

"We're fine, too!" Before Whitestar could speak, Vinetail's voice rang out as he wriggled free from a heap of snow. The rest of the ThunderClan cats tumbled out around him, shaking cold, wet clumps from their pelts and out of their ears.

"How can this be?" Whitestar whispered. "That branch fell on top of ThunderClan and ShadowClan; there was no room between them!"

Stonestar looked once more at the massive chunk of tree, then at the two groups of cats standing on either side, unhurt and exclaiming at their good luck.

"It's a sign from StarClan," Stonestar meowed, loud enough for his fellow leaders to hear but not the cats below. "StarClan is telling us that even when Clans are close together, they are separate, far enough apart for a tree to fall without touching them. Borders may be invisible and thin as a whisker, but they are strong as oak, and they cannot be crossed. Not for friendship, not for prey, not for anything."

Whitestar was nodding. "It's a sign," he said.

Brindlestar was staring in disbelief at the cats of her Clan. They were dazed and shocked but without injuries. Then she looked down at the fallen branch. "StarClan has spared my cats for a reason," she mewed.

"Find food in your territory," Stonestar urged. "Use the skills that only you and your Clanmates have—your cunning, stealth, ability to walk through the darkest nights. The prey is there, and you're the only Clan that can find it."

"You are right. StarClan must not wish us to take inferior food from inferior Clans." Brindlestar glanced at Whitestar, who wisely did not respond.

"Then it's decided," Emberstar meowed. "Another rule has been added to the warrior code. We must not hunt or trespass on another Clan's territory."

"Agreed," the other leaders mewed in unison. They dipped their heads to one another. "Until the next Gathering, may StarClan walk your path."

Hunting Fish!

Not all cats obey the code all the time.
For where there are young cats and a set
of rules to break, there is always
mischief brewing. . . .

"**O**uch! You're stepping on my foot!"

"Sorry!" puffed Dappletail. "I thought it was a pebble."

"Since when do pebbles have fur?" demanded White-eye, shaking her paw. She turned so that starlight glowed in her remaining eye; the other had been clawed out by a badger when she was an apprentice, blinding her.

Dappletail wriggled up beside her—on the side where White-eye could see. "Are we at the river?" she mewed.

White-eye shifted to make room under the ferns. "Yup. Look!"

Ahead of them, the ground was covered with small gray stones, sloping down to the thick black water that flowed swiftly by, sparkling with reflected stars.

"It's kind of spooky at night," Dappletail whispered, shrinking back against White-eye's sturdy shoulder.

White-eye gave her a nudge. "We'll be fine," she assured her. There was no way she was going back to the camp now. This was the biggest adventure she'd ever had! In fact, it was probably the biggest adventure any ThunderClan cat had had. They didn't *need* to take RiverClan's prey—it was greenleaf, and the woods were thrumming with juicy birds and squirrels—but White-eye wanted to know what fish tasted like, and why RiverClan was so snooty about its prey being the best of all the Clans'.

Dappletail jumped onto a flattened rock at the edge of the river and peered into the water. "I don't see any fish," she whispered. "Do you think they've gone to sleep?"

White-eye huffed impatiently as she squeezed onto the rock beside her. "Fish don't sleep!"

"They must," Dappletail argued. "Otherwise they'd be really tired."

"Well, maybe some of them are awake." White-eye wriggled forward until her front legs dangled over the water.

Dappletail eyed her dubiously. "Is that how RiverClan cats catch fish? You look like you're about to fall in."

"Look!" White-eye strained her neck out, her whiskers quivering with the effort. "There's something over there!" She tensed her hindquarters, and before Dappletail could say anything, she leaped off the rock with her front paws outstretched and plummeted into the water with an enormous splash.

Dappletail sprang back, blinking as drops flew into her eyes. She shook her head and stared at the river. The current flowed as swiftly as ever, but now it was carrying White-eye, gasping and scrabbling to keep her head above the surface.

"White-eye!" Dappletail wailed. "Come back!"

"I'm . . . trying . . ." came the muffled reply. There was another splash and White-eye's head bobbed under a wave as the water swept her around a rock.

Dappletail stood on the shore, her tail bristling with shock. "Help!" she yowled.

White-eye reappeared farther downstream. "Don't . . . tell anyone . . . we're . . . here," she spluttered. "Get . . . into . . . trouble. . . ."

"But you're drowning!" Dappletail shrieked. "Help!"

Somewhere in the forest an owl hooted, but there were no sounds of cats coming to help. Dappletail looked at the swift black river, took a deep breath, and ran into the waves. The water was so cold she couldn't breathe. Waves slapped around her, cutting her off from either shore and filling her ears with a deafening hiss.

Swimming's just like running, but in water, right?

She untangled her legs and tried to move them as if she were walking on grass, but as soon as she hauled herself upright in the water she sank and had to scrabble back to the surface, gasping for air. This was the worst idea White-eye had ever had!

"What in the name of StarClan is going on?"

An angry voice sounded above Dappletail's head, and she floundered around to see who was speaking. A brown-and-white tom was standing on a rock on the RiverClan side of the river, his eyes huge as moons.

"Help!" Dappletail yowled, before a wave filled her mouth and made her cough.

Another cat appeared beside the first one. "Owlfur, it's clearly not out for a nighttime swim. You'd better go fish it out before it drowns."

The brown-and-white tom slid into the water and his small head began bobbing steadily toward Dappletail. She kept her mouth shut and flailed with her paws, trying to stay in the same place. She winced as the tom clamped his jaws tightly in the scruff of her neck, and she felt herself being dragged through the water toward the shore. Her paws scraped against stones and she staggered out with most of the river streaming from her fur.

"My Clanmate!" she coughed. She twitched her tail downriver. "She's still in there!"

"Mouse-brains!" hissed the second cat. He braced his thick-pelted gray shoulders and headed for the river. "Owlfur, you stay here and make sure this feather-head doesn't try to follow me." He broke into a run and disappeared into the river, his pace staying the same even when he started swimming.

"You're from ThunderClan, aren't you?" Owlfur mewed disapprovingly.

Dappletail nodded, her whiskers heavy with drops.

"Let me guess. You were trying to steal our fish."

Dappletail's head drooped even lower. "S-sorry," she muttered.

The brown-and-white tom hissed, then raised his head. "Looks like Hailstar found your Clanmate," he meowed.

Hailstar? Oh, great. We've been rescued by the leader of RiverClan.

"Dappletail! Look!"

Noisy splashing behind her made Dappletail turn around. White-eye was stumbling out of the water with Hailstar shoving her from behind. Her pelt was slicked to her sides and her ears looked huge against her wet head, but his eyes shone as she dropped a twitching silver fish onto the stones.

"I caught a fish!"

Hailstar rolled his eyes. "You squashed it against a rock," he corrected. "And it wasn't yours to catch in the first place." His eyes narrowed. "You're trespassing and stealing. What do you say about that?"

"Hey! Are those our missing ThunderClan warriors?"

There was a shout from across the river. On the far shore, Pinestar and his deputy, Sunfall, were standing at the edge of the water, their fur frosted by starlight.

"We caught some unusual prey tonight," Hailstar called back. "Why not come across and see if it suits your appetite better?"

The ThunderClan cats ran along the shore and jumped across the stepping-stones, clearly visible in the low greenleaf river. Dappletail glanced sideways at White-eye as they waited for their Clan leader to arrive.

"I am never, ever listening to you again!" she hissed.

The four older cats stood in a line in front of Dappletail and White-eye and surveyed them.

"Just how many rules of the warrior code did you want to break tonight?" Pinestar began. "Trespassing, stealing prey, catching food for yourself . . . "

"I wanted to see what fish tasted like," White-eye mumbled.

Pinestar leaned closer to her. "We are from ThunderClan," he growled. "We. Don't. Eat. Fish."

Owlfur stepped forward. "Wait, I have an idea. Since these mouse-brains seem so determined to be RiverClan cats, why not let them eat their fresh-kill? After all, White-eye caught it."

Dappletail looked up in surprise. Weren't they going to be punished?

Pinestar's eyes gleamed. "What a good idea, Owlfur. White-eye, Dappletail, eat up. Don't waste a scrap, or that would be very insulting to your hosts."

White-eye didn't wait to be asked again. She opened her mouth wide and sank her jaws into the fish just behind its head. Feeling very uncomfortable with the other cats watching, Dappletail crouched by the tail of the fish and took a bite.

Yuck!

Both cats sprang back, their lips curling. Wet, cold, slimy, tasting of stones and weeds and mud . . .

Hailstar cocked his head on one side. "What's the matter?"

"It's disgusting!" White-eye spluttered.

Sunfall looked shocked. "You can't say that when RiverClan is so generously letting you eat your catch."

Dappletail forced herself to swallow and concentrated very hard on not being sick. "Please don't make us eat any more," she meowed.

Pinestar looked at them both. "The warrior code exists for a reason. ThunderClan cats don't eat fish, don't catch fish, don't swim, don't have anything to do with the river at all. RiverClan cats don't eat squirrels, so they don't live in the woods. ShadowClan cats don't eat rabbits, so they don't live on the moor."

Hailstar spoke up. "I think nearly being drowned is enough of a lesson for now. Go back to your Clan and leave the fish to us."

White-eye nodded hard. "No more fishing," she promised.

"No more adventures ever," Dappletail meowed. ThunderClan cats ate ThunderClan fresh-kill; as far as she cared, RiverClan cats could have all the fish in the world.

CODE THREE

*Caring for the weaker members of the Clan lies at
the heart of the way we live. We are taught to respect elders who
fought for the Clan in the past and kits who can't yet hunt for
themselves. However, moons ago, when the blood of warriors flowed
thick and fast over Sunningrocks, if you had asked a warrior
what he or she fought for, the warlike answer would have shocked
you. All that would change thanks to a visionary warrior
called Splashheart, who went on to lead RiverClan and bring
peace to the forest. Let me take you back. . . .*

A Mystical Battle

The shape was little more than a flicker beneath the surface of
the water, a trembling shadow cast on the stones crisscrossed
with waving green fronds. Splashheart kept absolutely still, waiting
for the fish to come closer. Another flicker, less than a tail-length
away, and Splashheart shot out one paw, his unsheathed claws
slicing through the cold water. When he felt his pad brush against
the fat, slick body, he curled his paw and swiped it toward him. The
fish flew out of the water, scattering silver droplets, and landed on

the bank beside him, where he finished it off with a swift blow.

"Good catch," said a voice behind him. It was Reedshine, the dark orange she-cat who had mentored him until two sunrises ago, when he received his warrior name.

"Thanks," Splashheart purred. "Want to share?"

Reedshine padded closer and sniffed at the fish before taking a bite. Splashheart bent down and took a mouthful from the other side of the fish. This was only his second catch as a warrior, and it tasted as good as the first.

On the other side of the river, Sunningrocks loomed, casting a heavy black shadow onto the water. These smooth gray rocks quickly grew warm in the sun, making them perfect to lie on and share tongues or just watch the river sliding past below. Some of RiverClan's elders could remember when the river flowed on the other side of Sunningrocks, cutting off RiverClan from ThunderClan's wooded territory. But then a great flood came one leaf-fall and the river burst its banks to surround the rocks, until they resembled a bleak gray island. When the floodwater went away, the river had carved a new course on RiverClan's side of the rocks. Before the next sunrise, ThunderClan had claimed Sunningrocks as its own, swarming across the dried-out riverbed to set scent markers along the new riverbank. The Clans had fought over them many times since, and at the moment the scent markers lay on the far side of the rocks, keeping ThunderClan firmly out.

Splashheart narrowed his eyes. There was a cat creeping along the far riverbank, head and tail low. The cat was half hidden by the shadow from the rocks, but it was a leaner, sleeker-furred shape than RiverClan cats, who grew plump and thick-pelted thanks to their watery prey. *ThunderClan!*

"ThunderClan intruders on Sunningrocks!" he yowled.

"I'll fetch help!" Reedshine told him. "Stay on this side of the river until I get back." She plunged into the reeds, her orange pelt quickly vanishing among the rattling brown stalks.

Splashheart's fur stood on end and his paws tingled. His first battle as a warrior!

"This is our territory now, fish-fur!" snarled a cat from the other side of the river.

"Never!" Splashheart hissed. He sank his claws into the edge of the bank, ready to leap into the water and start the battle on his own.

"Splashheart, wait!" Darkstar burst out from the reeds behind him.

Splashheart whirled around to face his leader. "We can't let them get away with this!" he protested.

The small brown she-cat met his gaze. "We won't," she promised grimly. Dry stalks rattled behind her and suddenly the bank was thronging with cats, warriors and apprentices, their fur fluffed up and their claws gleaming in the sun.

"RiverClan, attack!" yowled Darkstar, plunging into the river.

Splashheart scanned the rocks. Thank StarClan, they didn't seem to be outnumbered. Blackbee and Eeltail were chasing after a ThunderClan she-cat who was streaking for the cover of the ferns at the bottom of the rocks; Reedshine held another warrior in a paw lock, hissing a warning into his face. Darkstar had satisfied herself with a quick slash of claws across a dark brown cat's ears before standing back to let him run away, yowling.

As the warrior's screeches faded among quivering ferns, Splashheart heard a scraping noise from behind a tumble of boulders. He gathered his haunches beneath him and sprang onto the top of the nearest boulder. A pair of terrified amber eyes stared up at him from the other side.

"Don't hurt me!" bleated the small black-and-white cat—an apprentice, by the look of him.

"Then stay off our territory!" hissed Splashheart.

The ThunderClan cat didn't move. Instead, he curled his lip in a snarl. "Are you sure you want to threaten me, fish-fur?" he challenged.

Too late, Splashheart heard the scrape of claws on the rocks above him and felt a rush of air as two sleek-furred shapes landed, one at each flank. In a heartbeat, his face was thrust down against the rock. "Care to threaten us as well?" growled a voice in his ear, and the massive paw pressed harder on his neck.

"Get off him and fight a cat your own size!" screeched a voice from the riverbank. Splashheart caught a glimpse of dark orange fur leaping toward the boulders. Reedshine! She crashed straight into the warrior holding Splashheart down, and both cats plummeted into the narrow gap where the ThunderClan apprentice was crouching. The young cat jumped on top of Reedshine and began pummeling her belly with his forepaws; as Splashheart scrambled to his feet, he saw bright red streaks blossom in Reedshine's soft fur. He tried to jump down after her but the other ThunderClan warrior swiped his hind paws from underneath him and rolled him over.

The warrior loomed over him, her green eyes blazing. "StarClan changed the course of the river!" she hissed. "Sunningrocks belongs to ThunderClan now!"

"Never!" Splashheart spat, but the warrior pressed her paw against his throat and the sky began to go dark and fuzzy.

Suddenly there was a thud as two heavy bodies collided above Splashheart, and the weight on his throat lifted. He gulped down air, almost stopping when it felt like swallowing thorns.

"Don't just lie there, Splashheart," hissed Darkstar, who crouched on the rock beside him. "Get down to the shore with the others, quick." Splashheart sprang down to the stones at the edge of the water. The rest of the RiverClan warriors were huddled together, some of them belly-deep in water.

There was a scuffle behind him and Splashheart turned to see Darkstar half carrying Reedshine down the bank. The dark orange warrior left a trail of dark red smears behind her, and her eyes were half-closed. Splashheart raced over.

"Reedshine, wake up!" He looked at Darkstar. "We have to get her back to camp, now!"

Darkstar opened her mouth to let Reedshine sink gracelessly onto the stones. The leader's eyes were black with rage. "We will take her back," she promised. "But first, we will reclaim what is rightfully ours!" She raised her voice at the end so every RiverClan cat heard. They lifted their heads and stared at Darkstar in astonishment.

"But the battle is lost!" Eeltail spat. He jerked his muzzle toward the top of the rocks, where several ThunderClan warriors stood in triumph, their tails kinked high above their backs as they jeered at the defeated cats.

"It is only lost when we stop fighting!" replied Darkstar. She jumped onto the riverbank so all the cats could see her. "Our elders, and our elders' kin, and their kin before them, fought to keep Sunningrocks in our territory. Many of them lost their lives, giving up their last breath for stones that belong to us. Can we give up where they did not, turn tail and flee when they kept fighting so that their kits could hunt and play and bask on these rocks? Will you fight with me now, in honor of all our elders and all our unborn kits?"

"*We will fight!*" roared the RiverClan cats. In that moment,

Splashheart saw the rocks swarming with starry shapes of cats who had gone before him, his Clanmates from long ago battling over and over to keep Sunningrocks as their own. Now he would join them, set his paws where their paws once stood, and feel their battles echo around him as he proved himself worthy to walk among them.

With a single yowl, the RiverClan cats surged up the riverbank and onto the boulders. The ThunderClan warriors stood in a line on the far side of the summit, staring at them in astonishment.

"The battle is over," snarled one of them, a broad-shouldered tabby with amber eyes.

Darkstar faced him boldly, the fur standing up along her spine. "How can that be, when we are not beaten?" she challenged.

With a screech, the tabby sprang at her, but Darkstar sidestepped, spun around, and sank her claws into his back as he crashed to the floor. The RiverClan warriors leaped forward to meet the other ThunderClan cats, and Splashheart felt his teeth sink into short white fur. He didn't let go until he dragged the cat to the edge of the rocks.

"Go!" he ordered, releasing the cat's scruff at last. Without looking back, the warrior scrambled down the boulders and disappeared into the ferns at the edge of ThunderClan's territory.

"Good work," murmured a voice beside Splashheart. He had plunged back into the throng of cats, and for a moment he couldn't tell which cat was speaking to him.

"Watch out for that black-and-white tom over there," the voice continued, and Splashheart saw a ThunderClan warrior stalking toward Eeltail, who was holding down a spitting she-cat.

"Thanks!" he gasped and crossed the open ground in three quick strides, landing squarely on the black-and-white cat. Eeltail turned at the noise and lifted his paw so that the she-cat could flee; then he joined Splashheart and together they chased the black-and-white tom after his frightened Clanmate.

When the two cats had gone, Splashheart realized that the sounds of battle had grown quieter, muffled as if he were underwater.

"The battle has been won," whispered the voice. "Sunningrocks is safe."

Splashheart turned his head—the only part of his body he seemed able to move—and saw a faint, glimmering cat standing beside him. Her fur was the color of floodwater, almost black with streaks of pale gray, and her tail was so long the tip rested on the rock. RiverClan scent hung around her, but he'd never seen her before.

"Who are you?"

The cat dipped her head. "My name is Aspentail," she replied. "I am kin of your elders and of your elders' elders. I fought for these rocks once, and I will fight for them again, for as many moons as it takes, until ThunderClan learns that Sunningrocks belongs to RiverClan."

"I will fight with you," Splashheart vowed. Aspentail nodded and started to fade so that Splashheart could see the gray of the rock through her fur.

"Splashheart? Who are you talking to?"

Blackbee was standing behind him, looking puzzled. "Didn't you realize?" she demanded. "We won! Those fox-hearted ThunderClan cats won't set paw on Sunningrocks now."

"Not for this moon, at least," Splashheart whispered. "But if they do, we'll fight them again. Aspentail, too."

"What was that?" mewed Blackbee. "Are you okay, Splashheart? You're not wounded, are you?"

"No, no, I'm fine," Splashheart promised.

"Cats of RiverClan!" Darkstar was summoning her warriors to the center of the summit. "Sunningrocks belongs to us once more! And in honor of our elders and their kin before them, who never stopped fighting to defend our borders, we will catch fish on our way home and feed it to the oldest and youngest cats of the Clan. This victory is for them!"

Some of the warriors looked surprised, but Splashheart nodded. He would catch the plumpest fish he could find in memory of Aspentail and take it straight to the elders' den. And if he ever became leader of his Clan, he would make it part of the warrior code that elders and kits should be fed first, in honor of all they had done, and all they would do, for his Clanmates to come.

A Dark Path Chosen

*As you have seen, Clan cats are part of something bigger
than ourselves, and that ensures we are as strong as our strongest
warrior when trouble comes. But come see what can happen
if this part of the warrior code is ignored.*

Longtail winced as a cold drop of water splashed onto his neck. "The den is leaking again," he complained to Darkstripe, who was curled up beside him.

Darkstripe opened one yellow eye. "Better tell Redtail," he murmured. "He'll have to organize a cat to fix it before we drown in our sleep."

Longtail slid out of his nest, shivering as the bead of water rolled down his back, and pushed his way into the clearing. Leaf-fall was giving way to leaf-bare, and the sky was flat and gray like water. Longtail picked his way over to the cleft in the rock where he could hear Redtail, the ThunderClan deputy, speaking quietly with Bluestar. His words were punctuated with coughs that racked the warrior's body and left him breathless: The Clan was fighting off greencough, and Redtail had only just emerged from the medicine cat's den where he had been treated.

"We need to send out a hunting patrol," he wheezed to Bluestar. "The fresh-kill pile was ruined by the rain last night, and the sick cats won't get better if they're weak with hunger."

"Very well, but only send out healthy cats," Bluestar warned. "Which means you stay here, Redtail."

The deputy started to argue but was interrupted by another bout of coughing.

"Longtail!"

A tortoiseshell-and-white she-cat, her pelt dappled like a glade in greenleaf, was calling him from the shelter of a clump of ferns. Longtail changed direction to join her.

"What's up, Spottedleaf?"

"Has Redtail organized any hunting patrols yet?" The medicine cat's eyes were dark with worry. "I can't help sick cats when they're so hungry. I know hunting is hard in this weather, but we have to find them something to eat." Her bones shifted under her pelt as she moved, and Longtail guessed that Spottedleaf had been giving up her own share of fresh-kill to the cats she was trying to heal.

"I think he's just about to send one out," he told her.

"Good. Let's hope they come back quickly. Poppydawn is hardly strong enough to eat the catmint."

Longtail peered past her into the ferns, where he could just make out the dark red fur of the sick elder. Poppydawn told good stories and was popular with all the kits in the Clan because she let them chase her tail, which was as thick as a fox's.

Redtail nodded to Longtail, flicking drops of water from his feathered ears. "Are you free to go on a hunting patrol?"

"Yes," Longtail replied.

"Good. Take Darkstripe with you. Try Snakerocks—there might be some prey sheltering there. You shouldn't find any snakes at this time of year, but don't go too deep into the caves."

At least Darkstripe won't order me around, Longtail thought as he squeezed back into the warriors' den. In spite of the leaky roof, Darkstripe had gone back to sleep. Longtail prodded him with his paw.

"Wake up! We've got to go on a patrol."

Darkstripe raised his head and stared at him blearily. "In this weather? You must be crazy! Did you tell Redtail that the roof needs fixing?"

"I didn't get a chance," Longtail confessed. "Come on, it's just us. Redtail suggested we try Snakerocks."

"Great," Darkstripe grumbled, heaving himself to his paws. "I can either drown or get bitten for the sake of my Clan."

"It's not raining that hard," Longtail pointed out as they headed for the tunnel that led out of the camp. "It's mostly just water being shaken from the trees."

"Is that supposed to make me feel better?" Darkstripe muttered, but he sprang gracefully up the rocks that littered the side of the ravine and reached the top before Longtail.

The rain kept Twolegs and their dogs out of the woods, so the warriors had a clear run all the way to Snakerocks. Longtail shivered. Even if the snakes had gone for the cold season, this place still made him nervous. Darkstripe skirted the edge of the trees, sniffing at the dead bracken.

"I'm starving," he meowed. "We'd better catch something. I haven't found anything good on the fresh-kill pile for days."

Longtail headed for the pile of rocks, telling himself that he wouldn't go into any caves at all, not even a little way. His whiskers trembled as he picked up the scent of squirrel at the foot of the rocks. The trail led behind the stones and a little way into a clump of brambles. Crouching low, Longtail stepped paw by paw under the thorns. There was a patch of gray fur just visible through the tendrils. He gathered his haunches under him, wriggled to get his balance, then sprang. Blasting his way through the brambles, he landed squarely on the squirrel. Muttering a prayer to StarClan, and spitting out leaves, Longtail backed out of the thicket, dragging his fresh-kill.

"Good catch!"

Darkstripe was standing right behind him, making Longtail jump. The black-striped warrior padded forward, sniffing appreciatively. The squirrel's fluffy gray fur rippled under his breath. Darkstripe glanced over his shoulder. "This won't taste nearly as good once we've hauled it back to the camp."

Longtail shrugged. "We should catch something else quickly; then it will still be fresh."

"But it won't be as fresh as it is now." Darkstripe looked back at the squirrel. "And we'll hunt much better after a decent meal."

"The warrior code says we can't eat until the elders and kits have been fed," Longtail reminded him. His pelt was starting to prickle as if ants were crawling through it.

"How will any cat know?" Darkstripe murmured. He narrowed his eyes until they were tiny amber slits. "You won't tell, will you?" His voice was barely a whisper; Longtail could hardly hear him.

"I . . . I . . ."

Darkstripe opened his jaws and sank his teeth into the squirrel, without taking his eyes off Longtail. He chewed slowly, releasing the tempting smell of warm, plump meat.

We're as hungry as the rest of the Clan, and we need our strength to hunt. It makes no sense to let the warriors starve when they have to look after every other cat. I caught this squirrel easily; we'll catch plenty more.

Longtail bent his head and bit into the fresh-kill. Above him, a cold wind rattled the trees, and the rocks loomed gray and silent against the heavy sky.

Pelting rain made the sides of the ravine slippery, and the cats picked their way carefully down with their catch gripped in their mouths. Longtail had been lucky with the squirrel; prey had been much harder to find after that, and all they brought were two mice and an old, tough-looking blackbird. Neither cat looked each other in the eye as they dragged their fresh-kill over the muddy ground to the gorse tunnel. Darkstripe hung back, forcing Longtail to go first. The thorns seemed sharper against his pelt than before, and a feather from the blackbird had worked its way into his throat, making him choke and splutter through his mouthful. He pushed his way into the clearing and looked around, expecting to see a row of hungry cats waiting by the fresh-kill pile.

The clearing was empty, the ground shiny and bouncing with raindrops. Darkstripe joined Longtail and they stood side by side with their catch by their front paws. Before either of them could speak, a wail rose from the ferns around Spottedleaf's den.

"Poppydawn! No! Don't leave me!"

It was Rosetail, her daughter.

"It is her time to join StarClan. Our warrior ancestors are waiting for her." That was Spottedleaf, her voice muffled by grief.

Longtail looked at Darkstripe, feeling a wave of panic rise inside him. "We're too late! Poppydawn is dead! Spottedleaf said she needed to eat in order to fight the sickness, but we didn't come back in time! We should never have eaten that squirrel!"

"Shut up!" Darkstripe hissed. "What's the matter with you? Poppydawn was going to die anyway. We should let the old, useless cats go if it means the warriors survive. The Clan depends on us now, not them."

"We killed her. . . ."

"We did not! Greencough killed her. She was old and weak. We are the important cats; we should eat first. Do you want to do what's best for your Clan?"

"Of course . . ."

"Then you'll keep your mouth shut and let your Clanmates be grateful for what we brought back. There's one fewer mouth to feed now. Why spoil everything by trying to blame yourself for Poppydawn?"

But Poppydawn might still be alive if we had come back earlier—if we had come back with the squirrel.

Darkstripe was peering at Longstripe as if he could read his thoughts. "You'll keep quiet, won't you?" he hissed, and this time there was a hint of menace behind his eyes. "After all, I saw you eat that squirrel. I'll tell them what you did, how you insisted on stealing prey from the elders, how you refused to let me bring it back to the camp."

A hard, cold lump froze inside Longtail. "There's nothing to tell," he growled back. "We were sent to hunt for prey, and that's what we've done. No other warrior could have done better."

As he bent his head to pick up the blackbird and carry it to the fresh-kill pile, a waft of warm air ruffled his fur and a familiar scent brushed over him. Longtail lifted his head in horror.

Poppydawn! I'm so sorry!

Too late, came the silent reply. *Too late.*

CODE FOUR

*When you eat, whom do you thank for your food?
It was the clear-sighted leadership of Lilystar of ShadowClan,
moons ago, that taught us to respect our prey and helped us
to see how much we owe to our warrior ancestors for training us
and bringing us to a place where we can live like this.*

Mouse Games

"Over here, Fallowkit!" Driftkit dodged around a fallen branch and poked his head over the top to call to his sister.

Fallowkit popped up and shoved the mouse they were playing with toward him. Its limp body rolled over, leaving a faint mark on the boggy ground. The snow had only just melted and the ShadowClan camp was so wet, the kits' mother, Splashnose, spent every night licking the mud out of their belly fur. Driftkit scrambled onto the branch and launched himself off, landing flat on the mouse. It felt squishy under his paws, and it smelled of dirt and snowmelt.

Driftkit knew he was going to be the best ShadowClan warrior ever! He'd scratch out those scrawny WindClan cats' eyes, he'd chase the fat RiverClan cats until their legs fell off, he'd creep up on the ThunderClan cats and claw their ears. . . .

"Driftkit! What in the name of StarClan are you doing to that mouse?"

Driftkit fell off the mouse in surprise. A ginger-and-white she-cat with a bright orange tail was stalking toward him. "I was just practicing being a warrior, Sunnytail," Driftkit stammered to the ShadowClan deputy.

Sunnytail stared down at the mouse. "That's not fit to eat now! Does Splashnose know what you're doing?"

Fallowkit padded up, her light brown fur standing on end. "She's in the nursery. She told us to go outside and play."

Sunnytail shook her head. "This was the last piece of fresh-kill we had. Now the Clan will have to go hungry until the next hunting patrol."

"Sorry," Driftkit muttered. He wished a giant hole would open up in front of him so he could jump in and not be yelled at anymore. He was just having fun. He'd been stuck inside the den for moons because of the snow, and his legs felt as if they could run all the way to the Thunderpath that the warriors talked about.

The branches around the nursery rustled and a dusty-brown tabby with a white streak on her muzzle appeared. "What's the matter?" she called.

"Driftkit and Fallowkit have been playing with the last piece of fresh-kill, Splashnose," Sunnytail replied.

"I'm sure they didn't know it was the last piece . . ." Splashnose began.

"They must have known!" Sunnytail argued. "There would have been nothing left!"

"Is this true?" A pale gray cat padded up, her tail kinked

questioningly over her back. She looked from her deputy to Driftkit. "Did you take the last of our food?"

Driftkit tried to make a hole appear in front of his paws by staring at the ground really hard. Just his luck that Lilystar had overheard. "I guess," he whispered to the ShadowClan leader.

"It wasn't his fault," Splashnose put in, but Lilystar hushed her with a flick of her tail. When she spoke, her tone was unexpectedly gentle.

"Driftkit, you should not have taken that mouse to play with. Prey is too scarce to be wasted. That mouse did not die to become a toy, but to keep us alive after a long leaf-bare. Do you understand?"

Driftkit nodded without looking up. Beside him, Fallowkit squeaked, "Yes, Lilystar."

Suddenly a shadow swept over the clearing, and there was a strange rushing sound above Driftkit's head.

"Owl! Run!" screeched Splashnose, and the cats bolted for safety.

Driftkit was too terrified to move. He stared up at the huge white bird, which swooped closer and closer. He could see every feather on its chest, its sharp hooked talons, the ring of yellow around each eye as it glared down at him. He gulped, waiting to be swept up into the air.

The owl folded its wings at the last moment and dropped with its talons outstretched. Nearer, nearer . . . then it was pulling itself back up into the air with its mighty wings. Driftkit opened his eyes. He was still on the ground. The mouse had vanished; when he looked up, he could see its battered body dangling from the owl's claws, getting smaller and smaller as the bird disappeared over the trees.

I survived!

Splashnose raced up to Driftkit. "Are you all right, precious?" she gasped, sniffing him all over.

Driftkit shrugged away. Fierce warriors didn't get fussed over by their moms whenever they won a battle. "I'm fine," he muttered.

Lilystar pricked her ears to follow the path of the owl. "It is a sign," she declared. "StarClan gives our prey to us, and StarClan can take it away. We should give thanks to our warrior ancestors that we are able to eat at all. They provide every mouthful as well as our ability to hunt and feed ourselves. From the next Gathering, there will be an addition to the warrior code. Prey must be killed only to be eaten, and we must give thanks to StarClan for its life. This is the way of the warrior."

CODE FIVE

*It seems so obvious now that kits should not be allowed
to fight until they are properly trained and strong enough to
take on full-grown warriors. But it was not always like this.
It took the love of a mother cat to put a stop to
the destruction of fragile lives.*

The Queens Unite

"**A**ttack! Jump! Swipe! Roll! No, *roll.*"

Daisytail winced as Specklepaw scrambled to his feet and shook his head, panting. He looked dazed, and there was a bead of blood welling at the tip of one ear. His mentor, Slatepelt, nudged him toward the other apprentice in the training circle, Adderpaw.

"Try again," Slatepelt instructed gently.

Daisytail couldn't watch as Specklepaw launched himself at his rival. It seemed like only a moon ago that his freckled, pale brown head had nuzzled into her belly searching for milk. Adderpaw had been training for several moons longer and he looked full-grown next to Specklepaw, whose head barely reached his shoulder.

There was a thud behind Daisytail, and she bit her tongue to stop herself from wailing out loud.

"Did you see that?" Specklepaw called. "Did you, Mom? Did you? I pushed Adderpaw right over!"

Daisytail turned around and forced herself to purr approvingly. She could tell from the look exchanged by Adderpaw and Slatepelt that the older apprentice had deliberately let the little cat win. "Well done, nutkin," she called. A tuft of fur on Specklepaw's head was sticking up, and she longed to go over and lick it flat. "You'll be a warrior before you know it!" *Before my milk has dried up*, she added silently.

Slatepelt nodded to her. "He's learning fast. Which is good, because it looks like we'll be fighting ShadowClan again soon. They've been seen stealing rabbits in broad daylight, and Hazelstar won't let them get away with it."

Daisytail didn't answer. Her kit was too small to take part in a real battle. He couldn't even take on his own Clanmates, who would never try to rip his pelt, tear his eyes, claw his ears into shreds . . .

"Daisytail? Are you okay?" A dark brown face was peering anxiously out of the entrance to the nursery. Hawkfoot's three kits were half a moon younger than Specklepaw: They would be made apprentices any day now and kept bouncing around their nest practicing their battle moves.

"There's going to be another battle with ShadowClan," Daisytail burst out. "I can't let Specklepaw fight, I just can't!"

"You don't have a choice," Hawkfoot pointed out. "He's an apprentice now; this is what he's being trained for."

Daisytail lifted her head. "And if your kits are apprentices by then, will you let them go? Knowing they'll face blood-hungry ShadowClan warriors?"

Hawkfoot prodded a bramble tendril with her forepaw. "It's our duty to provide the Clan with new warriors," she mewed.

"And is it our duty to see those warriors die before they're full-grown?" Daisytail challenged. She turned and stalked away from the nursery.

"Where are you going?"

"To put a stop to this once and for all."

A bright orange sun stretched its paws over the edge of the moor, turning the sky above to pink and cream. Dew sparkled like starlight in the shadows cast by rocks and gorse bushes. On one of the rocks, Hazelstar stood to address his warriors. They stretched in a line on either side of him, facing the ShadowClan border, marked by a line of stunted trees.

"Warriors of WindClan!" Hazelstar cried. There was an indignant murmur from farther along the line, and Hazelstar's whiskers twitched. "And apprentices! ShadowClan has stolen from us one too many times! We will teach them that WindClan's borders are strong, they will be defended with claw and tooth, and our prey protected for our Clan alone."

The cats yowled in support, and the grass flickered with the shadows of lashing tails.

Like an echo, a yowl came from the trees on the other side of the border. The grass beneath the trees stirred, and a line of ShadowClan warriors stepped out. A white-furred cat with hard green eyes stood in the center. "Are you sure about that, Hazelstar?" he sneered. "Some of your warriors look awfully small."

His gaze swept over the smallest WindClan apprentices, who suddenly looked even tinier beside their Clanmates.

"I'd say we're evenly matched, Blizzardstar," Hazelstar replied calmly. He glanced toward the cats at the end of the ShadowClan line, some of whom still had a fuzz of kit fur around their ears.

Blizzardstar curled his lip. "We'll put that to the test, shall we?" he snarled. "ShadowClan, attack!"

"STOP!" Daisytail leaped onto the rock she had been hiding behind. Hawkfoot scrambled up beside her. "We won't let you fight!"

Blizzardstar stared at the queens in astonishment. "Are all your cats this scared of combat, Hazelstar?"

"It's not fear," called a cat from the ShadowClan line. She stepped into the open, her amber eyes reflecting the sun.

"Oakleaf? What in the name of StarClan are you doing?" Blizzardstar demanded.

Daisytail jumped down from the rock and padded into the open space between the battle lines. The grass felt cool and springy beneath her paws; she would not let it turn red with her own kit's blood. "We're stopping this battle," she announced. To her relief, her voice didn't give away how much she was trembling inside. "Some of these apprentices are barely weaned from their mothers' milk. They are too young to die, too young to fight, too young to be treated like full-grown warriors."

The ShadowClan queen walked out to join her. "Daisytail came to see me with her Clanmate Hawkfoot two sunrises ago. She told me that she didn't want to let her kit go into battle when he was too small to fight his own Clanmates, and she asked me if I would let my kit die like this, too." When Blizzardstar let out a questioning grunt, she turned and explained, "I met Daisytail once at a Gathering, when we had both just learned we were expecting kits. She remembered me and knew I would not want my kit to fight any more than she did."

Hazelstar turned to Daisytail. "What are you saying?" he queried, looking baffled. "That we should never fight again? Do you really think that is how the Clans could live?"

Daisytail shook her head. "No. I know battle is part of our life. It's what warriors train for. But they should only be asked to fight when they are old enough to stand a chance of winning. What is the point of training kits so young that they'll be lost in their first conflict?"

Out of the corner of her eye, she saw Specklepaw duck behind Adderpaw. Embarrassment prickled from every hair on his pelt, and he refused to meet her gaze. Inwardly Daisytail gave an amused purr. One day, he'd understand—he'd still be alive to know why his mother did this.

Oakleaf trotted across the grass and stood side by side with Daisytail and Hawkfoot. "We are united, Blizzardstar," she told him. She nodded toward the line, and several other she-cats padded out. Daisytail dipped her head to greet them; some of these queens were too old to have kits as young as hers, but they all felt the same: The youngest cats should not be expected to fight. The grass whispered softly as WindClan she-cats joined them, falling in beside their ShadowClan rivals.

Daisytail held her breath and looked from Hazelstar to Blizzardstar and back again. The leaders could still order their warriors into battle. All that would happen would be that she would be forced to watch her kit fall beneath the paws of a giant ShadowClan warrior, never to get up again.

"Hazelstar? Our queens have spoken." Blizzardstar stepped out from his battle line, looking hard at his rival leader. "Should we ignore them and fight?"

The ginger tom paused, letting his gaze rest on the group of she-cats before glancing at his tiny warriors. Then he faced

CODE FOUR

Blizzardstar again. "What sense is there in losing the future of our Clans, when if we let them grow stronger, battles will be more easily won?"

Daisytail almost purred out loud. Hazelstar had managed to make this sound like a threat to ShadowClan rather than a decision to decrease his battle line.

Blizzardstar nodded. "If you are going to remove your youngest cats, then so must I. ShadowClan cannot be accused of being unfair in battle."

"I would never suggest such a thing," Hazelstar murmured. He turned to Daisytail. "How do you propose that we make sure all Clans keep their youngest cats from battle?" he asked.

Daisytail gulped. Was she really being consulted by the leader of her Clan? She thought rapidly. "I think there should be an addition to the warrior code. That kits must be"—she looked up and down the battle line, judging which cats looked big enough to take on a fully trained warrior—"six moons old before they are allowed to train as apprentices."

Oakleaf brushed the tip of her tail against Daisytail's shoulder. "Until then, they must live within the camp, where the queens can be responsible for their safety."

Hazelstar nodded. "That makes sense to me. Thank you, Daisytail. And thank you, Oakleaf." He dipped his head to the ShadowClan queen. "Blizzardstar, are we agreed?"

The ShadowClan leader bowed his head. "We are. We will take this to the Gathering at the next full moon."

Daisytail gazed at Specklepaw, who looked ready to burst with frustration. *There will be other battles, my little warrior. But not yet. Not until you are ready.*

The Smallest Warrior

Only a leader that walks the blackest of paths
would break the code that protects kits. Brokenstar
of ShadowClan was such a leader.

The WindClan warrior sprang with his claws unsheathed, and the little black-and-white cat fell to the ground without making a sound. A trickle of blood crept from his ear, which was crumpled in the dust. Flintfang shook off the warrior trying to sink her teeth into his tail and bounded over to his unmoving Clanmate.

"Get off him, you mangy worm!" Flintfang snarled. Then he bent down to grasp Badgerpaw's scruff between his teeth. The apprentice's fur was still soft and fluffy, and it tickled Flintfang's nose. Blinking to stop the sneeze, Flintfang lifted the tiny limp body into the air and carried it to the edge of the WindClan camp. Behind him, screeches and thuds echoed around the shallow dip in the ground where WindClan had once made its home. Now all the dens were trampled and ruined, and the ground was sticky with blood. Brokenstar was right: This battle would force WindClan to leave the moor, and ShadowClan hunters would be able to take over the territory to feed their growing Clan.

But not Badgerpaw. His breathing was quick and shallow and a strange smell came from him, sour like blood and crow-food. There was nothing any cat could do to help him. Flintfang shook his head angrily. He had trained his apprentice in every battle skill he knew and made sure he could duck and roll and slash as well as any of the other apprentices. But Badgerpaw was only three moons old; he was too small to take on a full-grown WindClan warrior, his legs too short to reach the easily wounded parts of belly, eyes, and ears. What could a mentor do when he was expected to train a kit? The warrior code said that a warrior must be at least six moons old, but that didn't worry Flintfang as much as he feared Brokenstar. Flintfang had failed his leader—and Brokenstar would make sure every cat in the Clan knew. He turned away, ready to abandon his apprentice and teach that fox-faced WindClan warrior a lesson he wouldn't forget.

Badgerpaw's eyes flickered. "Flintfang? Is that you?"

Flintfang's heart sank. "Yes, it's me."

"Was . . . was I good enough?" Badgerpaw rasped in a tiny voice. His paws shifted in the dust and a bead of blood appeared at the corner of his lip. "I tried to remember everything you taught me."

Flintfang stared at the battered little body. Badgerpaw hadn't stood a chance from the moment the first battle yowl split the air.

"I hope Brokenstar is proud of me," Badgerpaw went on. His eyes were clouding over and starting to close. "And my mom."

Flintfang felt something stir inside him. What was he going to tell Fernshade? That her kit was always going to die in this battle because he was too small, too weak?

"Fernshade will be very proud of you," he meowed.

Badgerpaw opened his eyes with an effort and

looked straight at Flintfang. "Are you proud of me?"

Flintfang crouched beside Badgerpaw and stroked the apprentice's eyelids with the tip of his tail to close them again. "You fought brilliantly," he murmured.

"Will you be all right without me?" Badgerpaw asked fretfully. He moved his head and the trickle of blood coming from his ear thickened, spilling out faster.

"We'll do our best," Flintfang replied gravely. "And we'll always remember you and how brave you were."

Was it his imagination, or did the tiny black-and-white chest swell with pride?

"Do . . . do you think StarClan will make me a warrior now?"

Flintfang swallowed hard; there seemed to be a stone wedged in his throat. "I'm sure they will."

"What will my name be?" Badgerpaw wondered, his voice growing even fainter.

"I expect they'll let you choose your own name," Flintfang replied. The lump in his throat was growing, making it hard to speak.

"I'd like to be called Badgerfang. Like you, because you were such a great mentor."

Flintfang leaned forward and rested his muzzle on top of his apprentice's head. "That is a great honor. Badgerfang is a very good name for a warrior." He could feel Badgerpaw's breaths coming quicker now, his flank hardly rising at all as he fought for air. "You will watch over us from StarClan for all the moons to come." Badgerpaw let out a tiny sigh, and his flank stilled.

Flintfang straightened up. "This was not your time to die. For as long as I live, I will honor the warrior code and not train another kit who should still be at his mother's belly. Go now, little one, and walk with warriors."

CODE SIX

*Being a warrior isn't just about catching prey and fighting
other Clans, you know. It's about being part of a tradition that
stretches back longer than any cat can remember, and one
that will last for all the moons to come. It was a RiverClan medicine
cat who learned that the time when every cat realizes this most
is when they are first given their warrior name and become
responsible for the safety and survival of their Clan.*

A Night of Listening

"Meadowpelt! Meadowpelt, we need you!"

Meadowpelt put down the willow stick he was
shredding and wove his way between the pale yellow stalks that
shielded his den from the rest of the camp. It was greenleaf, and
for once the ground underpaw was dry and dusty rather than
pooling with water.

Several other RiverClan cats were in the clearing, looking
anxious as their Clannmates crackled nearer. Suddenly the
reeds rattled together and a small black tom burst out.

"Snaketooth is hurt!" he yowled.

"What happened, Molewhisker?" Troutstar demanded. Just then, two more cats appeared with a third propped between them, his dark brown head lolling and one of his hind legs trailing uselessly behind.

Troutstar glanced over his shoulder. "Meadowpelt, take over."

Meadowpelt ran forward to take a look at his latest patient. This wasn't the first injury he'd treated among these young warriors in the last moon. Molewhisker had ripped out one of his claws trying to jump across the river, and Lightningpelt, a light brown tabby with a distinctive white streak down her back, had nearly poked out her own eye chasing through the thickest part of the reeds. Every day, the warriors seemed to come up with yet another competition to discover who was the strongest, fastest . . . *or most mouse-brained*, Meadowpelt thought crossly.

Lightningpelt and Nettlepad laid Snaketooth on the ground in the middle of the clearing. Meadowpelt studied the twisted leg, noticing the way the snapped bone jutted out beneath the skin. There was a chance Snaketooth would never walk without a limp.

"What was it this time?" Meadowpelt sighed.

"Climbing one of the Great Oaks," Snaketooth muttered through gritted teeth. "I won."

"You should have seen him!" Lightningpelt burst out. "He practically climbed onto a cloud!"

"If I had seen him, I wouldn't have let him do something so utterly mouse-brained," Meadowpelt growled. "When will you learn to stop showing off and start putting your Clan first? At this rate there'll be no warriors left by leaf-bare." Lifting his head, he looked around and spotted Oatpaw, whom he was thinking of taking as his apprentice. "Oatpaw, fetch me some poppy seeds, will you?"

Oatpaw ducked his head and ran to the den, quickly returning with several tiny black seeds stuck to his forepaw.

"Lick these up," Meadowpelt told Snaketooth. He turned back to Oatpaw. "Help me carry him to my den. He'll need to stay there tonight."

Moonlight filtered through the reeds, striping the floor of the medicine cat's den with sharp, thin shadows. Meadowpelt checked that the reeds on Snaketooth's splint were bound tightly enough, and then padded heavily across the clearing to his nest.

The reeds slid apart and Molewhisker, Lightningpelt, and Nettlepad squeezed into the tiny space beside their sleeping friend. "We wanted to see if he was okay," Molewhisker explained in a loud whisper.

"That's up to StarClan now," Meadowpelt replied. "I've done as much as I can. Now go to your own dens and let him sleep."

It was too late. Snaketooth stirred and lifted his head a little way off the pillow of moss. "Hey, guys!" he croaked.

Nettlepad bent over him. "How's your leg? It looked really gross!"

Meadowpelt flicked his tail. "You can stay for a few moments, but no more, understand?"

The three healthy warriors looked at the medicine cat and nodded solemnly. With a grunt, Meadowpelt threaded his way between the reeds that circled his nest and settled down. Tired as he was—and getting a little deaf in his old age, he had to admit—he could still hear the warriors whispering to Snaketooth.

"You've got to get better real soon!"

"We're going to jump into the gorge on the full moon, remember?"

"Yeah, I dared you, so if you don't do it, I win!" That was Nettlepad, his voice rising with excitement.

"Hush!" Lightningpelt hissed. "Don't let every cat hear you! You know what the old ones are like—they never want us to have fun."

"They just wish they were young enough to jump into the gorge. But I bet they were never brave enough to try. Not like us!" Molewhisker sounded as if he thought he could grow wings and glide safely into the river as it thundered and foamed through the steep-sided canyon at the edge of their territory.

"Look, he's gone to sleep," whispered Lightningpelt. "Come on, let's leave him."

Meadowpelt listened to them padding away, bristling at their foolishness. His mind filled with shadows, and sleep was a long time coming.

"Troutstar? May I speak with you?" It was the following day, with hot, merciless sunshine bouncing off the reeds and the surface of the river.

The RiverClan leader opened his eyes from his doze. He was curled on a flat stone by the shore, his gray fur blending into the sun-bleached rock. "Is Snaketooth all right?" he asked anxiously.

Meadowpelt grunted. "You mean apart from having no sense at all? He'll live. But whether he'll be able to hunt and fight again, I'm not sure."

Troutstar shook his head. "I don't know why those warriors keep doing such ridiculous things."

"That's why I wanted to talk to you. I want to go to the Moonstone to ask StarClan for advice."

The gray cat looked at him in surprise. "Do you really think StarClan needs to be involved?"

Meadowpelt nodded. "Yes, I do. We have raised a whole generation of warriors who only want to amuse themselves. There aren't enough apprentices for them all to be mentors, so they're wasting time making up stupid, dangerous games. They've all been hurt, but it hasn't stopped them. Did you know they're planning to jump into the gorge on the full moon?"

Troutstar's tail bristled. "No, I didn't know that. Meadowpelt, if you think StarClan can help, then you must go. May StarClan be waiting for you with answers."

It was past nightfall by the time Meadowpelt reached the entrance to Mothermouth. The Highstones jabbed angrily into the sky, black against dove-gray. Meadowpelt let his mind empty as he felt his way down the long, dark tunnel. At the bottom, the flattened-egg moon made the Moonstone glow brightly enough to light up the chamber. Meadowpelt lay down at the foot of the Moonstone and pressed his muzzle against the sharp, cold rock.

"StarClan, please show me how to make my Clanmates understand that the Clan depends on them for its survival, and that they can't play like kits now that they are warriors."

He closed his eyes, and at once the scents of the riverbank brushed against his fur. He could hear the water rolling past, whispering against the stones, and the reeds rattling together as they were bent over by the breeze. When he opened his eyes, he found that he was lying in the center of the RiverClan camp with cats stirring softly around him, preparing for the night. With a shock, Meadowpelt realized that he didn't recognize any of them—no, it was more that he couldn't see them clearly enough, as if their faces were always in shadow and their scents too mixed by the breeze to distinguish one cat from another. Even their voices sounded muffled, almost familiar but not quite. He lay still with his chin on his paws and listened.

"We tracked that fox to the border, so hopefully it will stay away," one voice reported.

"I'm on dawn patrol tomorrow, so I'll look out for any new scents," came the reply.

"The elders are convinced it will come back once more," meowed another voice. "They said that foxes will check out a place twice before deciding whether or not to settle. I think we should take their advice and be prepared to chase it out again."

"I promised I'd take all the apprentices for a fishing lesson tomorrow. Could you do a hunting patrol in my place?"

"Sure. With those kits due any day, we're going to need a full fresh-kill pile. Have you seen how much the queens eat when they're nursing?"

There was a *mrrow* of amusement from the other cats, and Meadowpelt purred, too. Whoever these cats were, they were the kind of warriors RiverClan could be proud of: brave, loyal, hardworking, and aware of how much the whole Clan depended on them, from the frailest elder to the tiniest kit.

Warm dawn light roused Meadowpelt and he sat up, blinking, in the sunlit cavern. Was that it? He'd spent a night in his own Clan, listening to unidentified cats talk about their lives? *How is that supposed to help?*

There was the faintest echo inside his head: *A night in his own Clan, listening . . . But how does that provide me with answers for our mouse-brained warriors?*

Silence pressed on his ears. What was he going to tell Troutstar?

A night of listening . . .

To cats who cared about their Clan, who understood their duties and took pride in doing them well.

Is that what the warriors need?

Meadowpelt burst into the dazzling air and started to run down the rock-strewn hill. StarClan had given him the answer!

"One night? To think about being a warrior?" Troutstar sounded unconvinced, and Meadowpelt was starting to wonder if this wasn't such a great idea after all. Knowing the current RiverClan cats, they'd just come up with a bunch of games to play in the dark.

But Meadowpelt kept his doubts to himself. The full moon was only a day away, and with any luck a sleepless night would at least make the warriors too tired to carry out their mouse-brained scheme of jumping into the gorge.

The young cats looked startled when Troutstar explained what they had to do: spend one night in silent vigil, watching over the camp while their Clanmates slept. "And make sure you listen, as well!" he added sternly.

The sun was already sliding behind the outline of the Twoleg barns beyond the willow trees, so the Clan started to prepare for the night. Molewhisker, Lightningpelt, and Nettlepad stayed in the middle of the clearing, looking uncertain about what they were supposed to be doing. Meadowpelt couldn't blame them; he wasn't sure anymore that he'd understood StarClan.

Meadowpelt slid into his nest and gave in to a wave of black sleep.

"Fox! Wake up! Fox attack!"

Meadowpelt was on his feet and racing into the clearing before he had fully opened his eyes. The camp was bathed in cold white light and cats were plunging out of the reeds, hissing in alarm. Nettlepad stood in the middle of the clearing with his fur bristling.

"We heard a fox!" he gasped. "Creeping up on the nursery. Molewhisker and Lightningpelt have chased it away."

Troutstar nodded to a couple of senior warriors. "Go after them. Make sure they don't try to confront the fox. We just need it to leave the territory."

A white she-cat with splashes of ginger on her fur padded up to Nettlepad. A pair of tiny kits bundled along beside her. "You saved our lives!" she exclaimed. "Thank you!"

"I didn't even hear that mangy ol' fox creeping up on us!" squeaked one of the kits.

"Yeah, even though you've got really big ears!" taunted his littermate.

"Have not!"

"Have so! You look like a rabbit!"

Meadowpelt padded over to Nettlepad, who was looking rather uncomfortable at being the center of attention. "Sunspots is right; you saved her life and her kits'. You should be very proud."

Nettlepad shuffled his paws. "It's because we were being quiet, like you said. We'd never have heard that fox if we'd been in our dens."

Meadowpelt narrowed his eyes. "Or jumping into the gorge. Or climbing the Great Oaks at Fourtrees. Or chasing one another through the reeds, scaring off prey."

Nettlepad hung his head. "Yeah, I guess that was pretty mouse-brained."

Just then, Lightningpelt and Molewhisker hurtled back into the clearing, followed by the senior warriors. "We chased that fox all the way to the border!" Molewhisker panted, his eyes shining with triumph.

"It won't come back here in a hurry!" Lightningpelt declared.

"Don't be so sure," rasped Fernleaf, one of the elders. "Foxes have a habit of coming back once more before they decide whether or not to settle. You need to be ready to chase it off again."

Molewhisker straightened up. "No problem," he promised.

Lightningpelt spotted a row of apprentices peering out of their den. "Hey there! I know some great fishing techniques! Would you like me to show you them today?"

Nettlepad nodded. "She's really good, honestly. I'll do your hunting patrol for you, Lightningpelt."

"Thanks, that would be really helpful."

Meadowpelt stared. His vision was unfolding around him, faces and scents falling into place like raindrops. A night of listening had turned these cats into warriors that RiverClan could be proud of.

"Thank you, Meadowpelt," murmured a voice beside him. It was Troutstar.

Meadowpelt shrugged. "Thank StarClan," he mewed gruffly.

"At the Gathering tomorrow night, I'll suggest we add a new

part to the warrior code: that all new warriors must spend one night in silent vigil so they understand how much their Clan needs them now," Troutstar went on.

Meadowpelt nodded, and inside a small worm of pride stretched and swelled satisfyingly. *Yes, make it part of the warrior code, so that all cats have a night of listening. . . .*

Squirrelflight's Words of Wisdom

One day even you might have to sit vigil.
Here are a few tips from Squirrelflight to help you pass the night—if you're a ThunderClan warrior, that is!

A vigil is the proudest and scariest night of any warrior's life. It was for me! Having to spend a whole night awake guarding the Clan, trying not to doze off, jumping at every leaf fall in case it's an enemy attack, it's enough to send any cat running back to the nursery. So, I'm going to give you some tips on how to get through a vigil. That way you'll be prepared when it's your turn.

First, don't lie near the warriors' den; the noise of all that snoring will make you want to nod off. Or deafen you. If you feel sleepy, jump onto the Highledge—quietly, obviously, so you don't wake Firestar. I know, I know, we're not supposed to go up there, but it will give you a surge of energy and keep you going. When I kept my warrior's vigil, back in the old forest, I climbed onto the Highrock in the middle of the night and it was *amazing*. The camp looked so tiny!

And I thought about how brilliant it would feel to summon all the cats just by calling them together. . . . Don't look at me like that; you know I'd never have done something like that. Honestly.

Even if you don't go up to the Highledge, make sure you stand up and stretch every so often, otherwise you'll feel like you've turned into a lump of stone. A little game of mouse-chase won't offend the ancestors if it gets really cold. Just don't send it flying too close to the nursery, like I did, or you'll wake every kit. They can hear a game going on even when they're fast asleep! Trust me, the queens won't thank you for that.

If you hear or see anything suspicious, call out, "Who's there?" Even if it's just a cat coming back from the dirtplace, better to be safe than sorry. After all, tonight you're in charge! The safety of the whole Clan depends on you! Sorry, I'm really not trying to worry you. Let's hope nothing does happen, because after all you're not supposed to make any noise during the vigil. Unless there is a raid, in which case you must wake Firestar first, then the warriors. Don't investigate anything on your own; it's too risky. Obviously you're allowed to call for help if you need it. And you can drink if you get thirsty, but you mustn't eat. Your old mentor will come and tell you when the vigil is over, once the sun is up.

So, does all that sound okay? I haven't scared you, have I? Good luck! May StarClan watch over you!

CODE SEVEN

*Our skills and our knowledge will live forever,
thanks to our mentors, who teach the next generation of Clan cats
the way of the warrior. But it took a great leader to see
that it was not only the apprentice who gained valuable knowledge
from the mentor. Being entrusted with an apprentice teaches the
mentor how to lead and gain loyalty and respect. For what is a
deputy or leader if not a mentor to the whole Clan?*

Second in Command

"**S**tarClan, hear me as I make my choice. Acorntail will be
the new deputy of WindClan."

Featherstar stretched out and rested her muzzle lightly
on top of Acorntail's head. Acorntail
closed his eyes, swallowing his
grief for Pebblefur, the
cat who had once been
his mentor, and whose
death from a strange,

CODE EIGHT

agonizing lump in his belly had shocked the Clan.

"Acorntail! Acorntail!" called the cats behind him, but to Acorntail, they sounded flat and disappointed. It was obvious they didn't want him to be their deputy.

"Good luck, Acorntail," murmured a voice in his ear. It was Morningcloud, the dark gray she-cat who had made no secret of her surprise when Acorntail was picked for deputy instead of her.

"Thanks," Acorntail meowed. Behind her, he could see her apprentice Quickpaw glaring at him, his pale ginger face screwed up with indignation. Acorntail wondered if all young cats rewarded their mentors with such fierce loyalty. He hadn't yet had an apprentice of his own, so he didn't know what it would be like to train a new warrior and to watch him or her develop from bumbling kit to strong, skillful fighting cat.

Morningcloud padded back to Quickpaw, and Acorntail heard the young cat hiss, "It should have been you!"

The she-cat quieted him with a flick of her tail. "Maybe one day," she murmured softly.

"Acorntail, you need to sort out the patrols for today," Featherstar prompted. Her tone was almost apologetic, as if she didn't want to remind him of his duties.

"Oh, yes, of course," Acorntail stammered. "Gorseclaw, Sheeptail, and Cloversplash, you can go on hunting patrol."

Cloversplash, a lightly built dark brown she-cat with a white flash on her nose shaped exactly like a cloverleaf, stopped him. "We went on hunting patrol this morning. We should have a training session with our apprentices now."

Acorntail felt as if the three apprentices attached to these warriors were looking at him with a mixture of scorn and pity. He ducked his head. "Oh, yes, of course, training. Well, maybe you could take the evening hunting patrol?"

"Sure," mewed Thistlepaw, Sheeptail's apprentice. "We're always in the mood for chasing rabbits all over the place after fighting all afternoon."

Acorntail's fur prickled with embarrassment. Why didn't he think of that? Why was he being such a flea-brain?

"Right, okay. Morningcloud, could you and Quickpaw do a hunting patrol instead?"

Morningcloud put her head on one side. "On our own?" she questioned.

"Er, no. I'll come with you," Acorntail decided hastily. He glanced at Featherstar, who gave a tiny nod. Acorntail felt lower than a worm's belly. *Why did Featherstar make me her deputy when I'm so useless?*

"You'll do fine, Acorntail," Featherstar told him. She sounded tired and strained, and Acorntail realized how much she must still be grieving for Pebblefur, who had died only three sunrises ago. They were in her den, a shallow scoop in the sandy earth shielded by a wall of gorse. Sunhigh had just passed, and the hunting patrol was due to leave.

"Prey is running well at the moment. You'll catch plenty with Morningcloud and Quickpaw."

Acorntail heard the dismissal in her tone. He backed out of the den. Morningcloud and Quickpaw were waiting for him in the center of the camp. Quickpaw still looked hostile, but the she-cat's expression was impossible to read. Morningcloud just nodded and let Acorntail lead the way up the slope and out onto the moor.

Acorntail quickly detected the musky tang of rabbit and hurtled off. For the first time since being made deputy, he felt sure of what he was doing, confident in the swiftness of his paws and the prospect of a good piece of fresh-kill for the Clan. The rabbit tried to outrun him but he drew steadily alongside, pounced from running full speed, and brought it down with a muffled snap of neck bones. He lifted his head and looked around. Morningcloud was racing after a young rabbit, her tail bouncing as she tore across the warm grass, and Quickpaw was sniffing the ground as if he had picked up the scent of a plover's nest. Eggs laid in a scoop of earth were a rare treat for the cats as plovers defended their unhatched young fiercely, but Quickpaw already had a reputation not just for tracking the nests but for carrying the eggs undamaged back to camp, tucked under his chin. Acorntail felt a little pebble of worry in his stomach dissolve. His Clan was the best by far, and it was an honor to be their deputy.

He stiffened. There was another scent on the air, not rabbit or freshly laid eggs, but feline. The breeze was carrying it from the direction of Fourtrees and the border with ThunderClan. What did those mangy tree-dwellers want now? They were far too slow and fat to catch WindClan's prey, so why would they even try?

His fur bristling, Acorntail shoved his rabbit under a gorse bush and trotted toward the border. The scent grew stronger. As he crested a rise close to the edge of WindClan territory, he saw three ThunderClan cats walking along the border, barely a whisker-length from trespassing.

"Did you want something?" he growled.

The biggest ThunderClan cat shook his head. "Just doing a patrol," he replied indifferently.

Acorntail looked closer. The smallest cat, which looked like an apprentice, had a tuft of dusky-brown fur stuck on his nose. There was only one type of prey that had fur like that.

"Have you been stealing rabbits?" Acorntail hissed.

The apprentice's eyes stretched wide—in guilty horror, Acorntail was sure—but the big warrior just curled his lip. "As if we'd waste our energy chasing your scrawny prey."

Acorntail opened his jaws; he could clearly taste the scent of fresh-killed rabbit clinging to these cats. Before he could say anything, Morningcloud and Quickpaw hurtled up from farther along the border.

"We found a dead rabbit!" Quickpaw panted.

"With ThunderClan scent on it," Morningcloud added. She skidded to a stop and narrowed her eyes at the rival patrol.

Acorntail flattened his ears. "So you did steal our prey!"

"It was dead already," growled the ThunderClan warrior. "We know better than to waste good fresh-kill—unlike your Clan."

"It did look old and it smelled funny," Quickpaw meowed before Acorntail could silence him. "It could have been dead for days. Yuck, you just ate crow-food!"

"That's not the point!" Acorntail hissed. *What kind of deputy lets the first rival patrol he meets get away with trespassing and theft?* "These cats have stolen our prey! They must be taught a lesson! WindClan, attack!"

He sprang at the big ThunderClan warrior, claws unsheathed. To his surprise, the warrior didn't try to jump away or fight back. Instead, he stared past Acorntail with a glimmer of amusement in his eyes. Acorntail thudded to the ground and looked over his shoulder.

Morningcloud and Quickpaw were standing close together, watching him.

"Attack!" yowled Acorntail.

"Don't be such a mouse-brain," Morningcloud retorted. "I'm not putting my apprentice in danger for the sake of crow-food. If they want to eat rotten prey that will give them bellyache, that's up to them."

"But they trespassed!" Acorntail protested, starting to feel like the day couldn't get any worse.

"Actually we didn't," the other ThunderClan warrior put in helpfully. "The rabbit was on our side of the border."

Acorntail looked questioningly at Morningcloud. She nodded.

"Why didn't you tell me?" Acorntail demanded.

"We were going to," Morningcloud replied. "You didn't give us a chance."

"And now I think you'll find you're trespassing on our territory," the first ThunderClan warrior pointed out.

Acorntail walked stiffly back across the border. "Morningcloud, Quickpaw, we're going back to the camp," he announced. "Featherstar needs to be told that a rabbit has died on ThunderClan's territory."

CODE
7

Morningcloud looked faintly surprised, but to his relief, she didn't argue.

"Which means it belonged to us anyway!" called the ThunderClan warrior as they headed back up the hill. "You should pick your battles more carefully."

I don't know enough to be a deputy, Acorntail thought miserably. *I'm going to tell Featherstar I can't do this.*

"You've made a mistake. You'll have to choose another cat to be deputy."

Featherstar regarded him from her nest, her blue eyes glowing in the half-light behind the gorse bushes. "When you became an apprentice, did you know all the fighting moves and how to hunt prey?"

"Of course not," Acorntail replied, puzzled.

"And when you became a warrior, did you know how to lead patrols, how to find the best places to hunt, and where our rivals were most likely to try to cross our border?"

Acorntail shook his head.

"Then why do you expect to know everything about being a deputy on your very first day? Every cat knows you have things to learn, but once you have, you'll be as good as Pebblefur."

Never.

"Think back to when you were an apprentice," Featherstar went on. "Remember what it was like to learn new things every day, knowing they would all lead to making you a warrior of WindClan?"

"But that was different," Acorntail argued. "I didn't have responsibility for the whole Clan then."

"And you don't now," Featherstar pointed out. "I'm still the leader." She put her head to one side. "Why do you feel that you're not worthy of giving orders to your Clanmates, Acorntail?"

"Because I don't know how to! Look at what happened today: Morningcloud would never have given the order to attack. She'd have found out all the information first, and then made sure that her apprentice wasn't in danger if a fight started. She'd make a much better deputy than me."

"But I chose you," Featherstar meowed. She was silent for a while, and Acorntail tried not to fidget. Then she lifted her head and looked straight at him. "I'm sorry. I should have given you an apprentice first. You would have gotten used to giving orders, and you would understand how protective mentors feel about sending young cats into battle."

She sounded so flat and defeated that Acorntail felt a rush of concern for her. She had lost her last deputy, now making her life even more difficult.

"It's not too late," he meowed firmly. "Give me an apprentice now, and I can learn. Cherryfeather's kits are nearly six moons old; let me have Pricklekit."

Featherstar held his gaze. "If I do that, will you stay as my deputy?"

Acorntail nodded. "I'll be the best deputy I can be. Pebblefur would have wanted me to do that."

"And you'll be as good a mentor to your apprentice as he was to you," Featherstar assured him. She went on, "I think I'll suggest an addition to the warrior code at the next Gathering, that a warrior cannot be made deputy unless he has had an apprentice."

Acorntail winced, and she added quickly, "Not because I regret choosing you, Acorntail, but because you're right. Training an apprentice teaches a cat how to give orders, how to protect the less-experienced fighters, and establishes bonds of loyalty that can survive the worst battles.

CODE
7

"Now, go sort out the dawn patrols for tomorrow. And then you might like to visit the nursery to see how your future apprentice is faring!"

CODE EIGHT

*At the dawn of the Clans, new Clan leaders were chosen
from the kin of the previous leader: often their kits, but sometimes
their littermates or their kits' kits. Leaders were well respected
enough that their kin was respected, too, by the whole Clan, and it
seemed the easiest way to choose a new head of the Clan. But not all
cats follow their kin in skills and temperament, and as you will see,
not every new leader was well suited or well received.*

Follow My Leader

The air stilled until the trees were silent, and the only sound
was the splash of water over stones. The brown tabby cat lay
in the shelter of thick ferns, his breathing so shallow that his flank
barely stirred.

"Robinwing?" he rasped.

"Yes, I'm here, Beechstar." Robinwing leaned closer, refusing
to flinch away from the stench of death that already clung to the
old cat's fur. "Your Clan is safe."

The tip of Beechstar's tail twitched. "They won't be safe for
long. RiverClan will not be content with my death. SkyClan must

attack again before they do. Take the battle into their territory this time. And make sure we win."

"Hush, Father," urged Mothpelt. "Get some rest, and we'll take you back to the camp tomorrow."

"This is my final rest," Beechstar whispered. "My ninth life is slipping away; my warrior ancestors are already waiting for me." His milky blue gaze focused on a point past them; Robinwing instinctively turned to look, but there was nothing except trees and bracken. "I come, my friends. Wait just one moment longer." With an effort, Beechstar dragged his gaze back to the black-and-brown cat beside him. "Lead our Clan well, Mothpelt. Make me proud as I watch you from StarClan."

"Father, no!" Mothpelt yowled, but the leader's eyes were closing now and his legs relaxed as he surrendered his final life.

Robinwing exchanged an agonized glance with a third cat watching the tragic scene: Maplewhisker, SkyClan's deputy. He knew she shared his concerns about Mothpelt as a leader. They had shared the nursery with him, trained side by side to become warriors, and seen him struggle to mentor a succession of apprentices.

CODE
8

Maplewhisker fell in beside Robinwing as they walked back to the camp to fetch the elders who would bury Beechstar. "No cat can doubt his loyalty to SkyClan and to the memory of his father," she pointed out, even though Robinwing hadn't said a word. "And he fought as bravely as any of us yesterday, especially after his father fell."

Robinwing didn't reply. He wanted to give Mothpelt a chance to show he could lead SkyClan—for the sake of his Clanmates. They were still at war with RiverClan over the territory on the SkyClan side of the river, and he needed to be at least as strong and wise as his father.

"He will need our support," Maplewhisker went on.

Robinwing glanced sideways at her. "Even if we don't agree with him?"

Maplewhisker flicked her ears. "He is our leader now. StarClan will guide his paws."

"Let all cats old enough to catch their own prey gather to hear me!"

It was raining hard, and Mothpelt had to raise his voice to be heard above the thundering of water through the trees. His father had been buried the day before, and he would be going to the Moonstone to receive his nine lives and his new name that night.

"Cats of SkyClan! My father's last wish was that we take the battle to RiverClan's side of the river and prove once and for all that SkyClan cannot be beaten!" Mothpelt declared.

There were yowls of support from the cats huddled below the branch where he balanced. Robinwing kept quiet. He was wondering what the river looked like after all the rain.

Mothpelt leaped down from the branch and ran to the entrance of the camp, his tail waving. "I will lead my warriors into battle, to honor my father who was the greatest leader SkyClan has ever known!"

And who would know better than to set out before checking the height of the river, Robinwing thought.

The warriors streamed out of the camp, apprentices racing to keep up without tripping over branches brought down by the weight of sodden leaves. Storms this late in greenleaf were dangerous because water wasn't the only thing to fall from the sky. Robinwing dropped back to give his own apprentice a shove over a slippery tree trunk. Rubblepaw's fur was slicked to his sides, black with rain and streaked with mud and scraps of moss.

Rubblepaw looked up at Robinwing and blinked raindrops

from his eyes. "I feel like I'm going to drown before I get to the river!" he spluttered.

And I'm afraid you'll drown when you get there. "You're doing great. Just follow the warriors," Robinwing told him. Picking up his pace, he squeezed past the other cats until he was at the front, next to Maplewhisker.

"What do you think the river's like today?" he asked as quietly as he could between panting for breath.

She gave a tiny shake of her head. "We'll see when we get there."

Suddenly they burst out of the trees and their paws crunched on pebbles that sloped steeply down to the edge of the water. Robinwing stopped and stared in horror. The river was swollen to twice its size; the shore was no more than a narrow strip of pebbles, barely a fox-length wide, and the crossing stones were marked only by flashes of white water where the waves broke over the top.

"SkyClan, attack!" yowled Mothpelt, rushing toward the river.

Robinwing glanced at Maplewhisker, who looked as horrified as he felt. RiverClan wouldn't need to fight them; they could just sit on the far bank and watch the floodwater carry the SkyClan cats away. Beechstar would not have wanted his Clan to die like this!

"Mothpelt, stop!" Robinwing screeched. He flung himself across the stones and brought his Clan leader crashing down, careful to keep his claws sheathed.

"What in the name of StarClan . . . ?" spat Mothpelt. "Robinwing, let me go! Since when were you such a coward?"

Robinwing let his leader stand up, but positioned himself between Mothpelt and the river. Behind the leader, the SkyClan cats lined up, their expressions ranging from angry to bewildered to relieved. "I won't let you cross the river," Robinwing meowed. "It's too dangerous."

"Get out of my way," Mothpelt growled. "Or have you turned traitor and joined RiverClan?"

"I am as loyal to SkyClan as I ever was," Robinwing replied, keeping his voice even. "Too loyal to watch my Clanmates drown before they have a chance to fight. We can fight this battle another day."

"No! This battle will be fought now, before the memory of my father fades in our hearts. His death must be avenged!"

"Not if it means other SkyClan cats die!" Robinwing protested, but Mothpelt was already pushing past him and plunging into the water. Almost at once, a wave broke over his head and he disappeared, but then he bobbed up farther into the river, his ears twitching as he struck out for the first crossing stone. White water spat in his face but he screwed up his eyes and clung to the rock with his claws until he could drag himself onto it and stand belly-deep in churning foam.

"Come on!" he yowled. "All those SkyClan cats who wish to avenge our leader's death, follow me!"

Robinwing watched helplessly as at least half of his fellow warriors and their apprentices ran past him and splashed into the river.

"No!" he yowled, watching as they floundered in the icy water.

Robinwing turned to face Maplewhisker, reading in her eyes that she was torn between loyalty to her leader and fear for her Clanmates in the swollen river. "It looks like Mothpelt is all right for now, as long as he stays on that rock," Robinwing meowed. "We'll have to get the others out before they go under."

The cats who hadn't rushed into the river were creeping forward, their eyes huge as they watched their Clanmates struggle. Rubblepaw came up to Robinwing. "We have to help them!" he gasped.

"Yes, we do," Robinwing agreed. "Maplewhisker, do you agree?"

She nodded. "Warriors and apprentices of SkyClan!" she called, addressing the cats on the shore. "Our Clanmates are in danger from the flooded river. No cat must go into the water without having two other cats in a chain behind. No apprentices must go near the water. Rescue the cats closest to the shore first; don't take unnecessary risks." She glanced at Robinwing. "Do you think that will work?"

"Definitely." He touched her shoulder with the tip of his tail, wanting to know how proud he was of her right now. "I'll form a chain with Rubblepaw and Spiderpelt. You stay on the shore and watch out for cats who need help most quickly." He watched her run along the shore, encouraging cats to join into chains. Then he flicked his tail at Spiderpelt. "Come on. You take my tail, and Rubblepaw will take yours."

CODE
8

"Ready?" Robinwing called, and the other cats nodded. Taking a deep breath, he jumped over a wave and landed up to his chin in icy cold water. He flailed his legs, pulling himself toward the middle of the river. On either side of him, other warriors did the same, their necks strained to keep their muzzles above the surface. A red-brown shape bobbed on the other side of a wave. Robinwing held his breath as the wave swept over his head, then struck out toward the shape. It was Squirrelfur. His eyes were closed and he looked exhausted as he battled to stay afloat.

"Don't struggle," Robinwing panted before biting deep into Squirrelfur's scruff. At once, he felt his tail being tugged, and he was pulled back toward the shore, dragging Squirrelfur with him. Maplewhisker was standing belly-deep at the edge of the river; she grabbed Squirrelfur's scruff on the other side and nodded to

Robinwing that she had a firm hold on him. Robinwing plunged back into the river.

One more warrior and two apprentices soon stood shivering on the bank, with Rubblepaw glaring sideways at them as if he held them responsible for his mentor risking his life to save them.

"You've done enough," Maplewhisker urged Robinwing as he crouched on the stones, coughing up river water. He shook his head.

"I have to fetch Mothpelt," he gulped. The leader was still clinging to the crossing stone, watching silent and wide-eyed as his Clanmates were rescued from the angry river. Robinwing knew he would be too cold and exhausted to make it back to the shore without help.

"Promise me one thing," he meowed. Maplewhisker looked puzzled. "Promise me you'll be the new leader of SkyClan."

"I can't do that!" Maplewhisker protested.

"You have to. And with the support of your Clanmates, you will," Robinwing told her. He flicked his tail at the cats around them, staggering onto dry ground with grateful glances at their deputy for organizing the rescue patrol.

"I'll support you," Spiderpelt offered.

"And me," Rubblepaw put in.

"Our Clanmates aren't mouse-brained," Robinwing murmured. "They respected you as their deputy, and they'll respect you as our leader. And they'll respect Mothpelt as a warrior."

Maplewhisker looked once more at her sodden Clanmates, then nodded. "And I'm not mouse-brained enough to think that my Clan doesn't need me. If Mothpelt agrees, then I'll lead SkyClan."

"In that case, we'd better fetch him," Robinwing meowed. He glanced at Spiderpelt and Rubblepaw. "Ready?"

"Lead on," Spiderpelt meowed, and Robinwing plunged back into the waves. SkyClan would be safe under Maplestar's leadership. And Robinwing would suggest that a new rule be introduced to the warrior code: that deputies replaced leaders when they lost their ninth life, as the cats most used to leadership and dealing with rival Clans.

Too Late for Regrets: Tallstar Explains

In StarClan there is plenty of time for fallen leaders to think over the decisions they made when they ruled their living Clanmates, and there is no escaping judgment as they watch over the consequences. Listen as Tallstar, the fallen WindClan leader, talks to Bluestar about one such decision, still hoping that it was the right one.

CODE
8

Bluestar? May I speak with you, my friend? My thoughts trouble me and keep me from sleeping.

You think I made a mistake, don't you? You may shake your head, but I can tell by your eyes that you're afraid of what I have done. Would you have let Mudclaw take over your Clan? Why? Because it was the only way to fulfill the warrior code and the expectations of all your Clanmates? But my vision, Bluestar, I cannot forget my vision. I dreamed of a hillside stained with blood, of cats

wailing for their kits and of warriors who had to watch their life drain out onto the grass. I could not tell who was fighting whom, just that every cat in WindClan had suffered a loss from an unjust battle. And looking down on it all from the crest of the hill was Mudclaw—Mudstar, now, leader of WindClan—because I had let him remain as my deputy. How could I let that happen?

I know my Clanmates assumed my reasoning was muddled because my final life was slipping away. Even your Clanmates Firestar and Brambleclaw looked at me with pity as they pretended to support my change of heart. I didn't have enough breath, enough words left to explain what I had just seen behind my closed eyes. I died knowing that my Clan might hate me for changing everything so late—and knowing that I had no choice. Onewhisker would have been as good a deputy as Mudclaw, and he will make a great leader.

I know you think that I'm an arrogant old cat who has made everything much, much worse by giving my Clan a leader they were not prepared for. But it was the only way to save them!

I know that WindClan will be safe under Onewhisker. He will have to prove his strength one day; every leader does. And if I was wrong, if I should have let Mudclaw succeed me because he was my deputy first, then it's too late. What's done is done. I didn't come to StarClan to regret my last decision as leader of WindClan. Whatever happens, it cannot be worse than the fate WindClan would have suffered if Mudclaw had remained.

CODE NINE

*It may seem callous to cats like you that a new deputy
is named over the body of the old one. Would you prefer to grieve
for one cat before passing your loyalties to another?
As you are about to see, dwelling in the past is not a luxury
warrior cats have; we must face the future.
The time for mourning will come.*

A Sign from StarClan

Redscar studied the spluttering, hunched cat in front of him
and shook his head. "You can't go to the Moonstone today,
Brightwhisker. You wouldn't make it as far as the Thunderpath."

Brightwhisker paused to gulp in air, then protested, "But I
have to go! I have to receive my nine lives and my new name from
StarClan!"

"StarClan will be perfectly aware of how sick you are," Redscar
pointed out. "They won't want you to exhaust yourself so soon.
Your Clan needs you whole and well. They have already accepted
you as their leader."

The brown-and-white she-cat's eyes clouded. "They mourn for Snowstar as much as I do. I wish I was still his deputy."

"Snowstar will be mourned for many moons, but that can't stop us from doing our duty. And yours," Redscar added, "is to get rid of this whitecough so you can be fit and strong to lead your Clan."

"Are you sure it's whitecough? Could it be greencough, like Snowstar had?"

"It's whitecough, definitely," Redscar meowed. "Now, lie down and rest."

"But I need to appoint a deputy, too," Brightwhisker protested, lapsing into a fit of coughing.

"It can wait until you can do it without coughing in his or her face. I'll bring you some tansy to soothe your chest and a poppy seed to help you sleep."

When he returned, Brightwhisker was curled in her nest, her flank rising and falling evenly. She didn't stir, so he decided not to wake her. He left the tansy leaves and the poppy seed beside a clump of moss soaked with water. Stretching the stiffness from his legs one paw at a time, he picked his way across the rutted, half-frozen clearing and headed for his nest of crow feathers and dry bracken. Darkness claimed him as soon as he closed his eyes.

"Redscar! Redscar! Come quickly!"

Redscar shot out of his nest and pushed his way into the open. Flowerstem was staring at him as if all the foxes of the forest were on her tail. "I can't wake Brightwhisker!" she wailed.

Every hair on Redscar's pelt stood on end. He'd left her only one poppy seed, barely enough for a whole night's sleep.

"Come see," Flowerstem pleaded, but Redscar was already pushing past her, heading for the leader's den. It was dark inside, and Redscar had to blink and wait impatiently for his eyes to adjust. Slowly he made out Brightwhisker's sleeping shape. She didn't seem to have moved since he last checked on her.

Oh, StarClan, don't let her be dead!

Redscar pushed his nose into her neck fur, but there was no sign of the telltale throb of life beneath the skin, and her fur was as cold as frost.

"Redscar?" Flowerstem was standing in the entrance to the den.

He turned to her and shook his head. Another leader had died, before she'd had a chance to receive her nine lives.

"Oh, no!" Flowerstem wailed.

A tortoiseshell head appeared behind her. "What's wrong?"

"Oh, Mossfire!" Flowerstem turned to face her littermate. "Brightwhisker's dead!"

Redscar padded out of the den, his paws heavy as stone. "She must have developed greencough in the night. She died in her sleep."

Mossfire stared at him. "But . . . she never chose a deputy! Who will be our leader now?"

Redscar knew he had to help his Clan find a way out of this terrible darkness. "I'll call the cats together," he meowed.

He chose to stay on the ground rather than stand on the fallen log that the leaders had used to address the Clan. Brightwhisker had taken her place there only once, to greet her Clan for the first time since Snowstar's death; a fit of coughing had stopped her, and Redscar had ordered her back to her den. *I should have known it was greencough! There must have been something else I could have done.*

Like let her appoint a deputy? a small voice inside him challenged.

Redscar pushed it away. "Cats of ShadowClan, Brightwhisker is dead. There will be time to grieve for her, but first we must choose a new leader. Are there any cats who wish to volunteer?"

His Clanmates shifted restlessly and there were worried murmurs, but no cat spoke out until Jumpfoot stepped forward. His muscles rippled under his black pelt, and his green eyes were somber. "I will lead ShadowClan, if my Clanmates wish it."

There were several yowls of approval, but some murmurs of disagreement. "We think Mossfire should be leader," called one of the queens. "Jumpfoot is too quick to go into battle. We want peace for our kits."

Mossfire walked forward to stand beside Jumpfoot. She dipped her head to Redscar. "My Clanmates honor me, and I would be willing to be their leader."

"Not all of them want you," snarled Jumpfoot. "Who'd want a Clan full of cowards, too frightened to defend their borders?"

"Not rushing into every battle doesn't make me a coward," Mossfire retorted. "I can fight as well as you any day."

"Prove it," Jumpfoot challenged.

"This is no way to choose a leader!" Flowerstem cried.

Jumpfoot glared at her. "We'll fight, and whichever cat StarClan favors will be victorious."

Flowerstem looked pleadingly at Redscar, but he felt frozen. What was happening to his Clan?

Jumpfoot and Mossfire started circling each other; the other cats moved back to give them more room. Mossfire struck first, with an easy swipe that Jumpfoot sprang away from with a contemptuous hiss. "You'll have to do better than that!"

"Very well," spat Mossfire, and she leaped at him, front legs outstretched, claws glinting in the frosty sun. She raked a set of scratches into Jumpfoot's flank, leaving scarlet beads of blood. With a yowl, Jumpfoot spun around and slashed at her face, then sank his claws into her shoulder and rolled her onto the ground, pummeling at her with his hind legs.

Redscar turned away. He could not believe StarClan wanted two warriors to fight like this in order to lead their Clan. He winced as he heard Mossfire gasp with pain and the sound of ripping fur as she retaliated. There was a thud as Jumpfoot went down and a gasp from the watching cats. Then another, softer thud as Mossfire crumpled beside him.

"Mossfire! No!" That was Flowerstem.

The stench of blood told Redscar what he would see. He turned around. The two cats were lying still as their lives ebbed away from blows struck too close, too hard. Redscar felt numb. He had failed, again.

Three elders were already shuffling forward to rearrange the bodies for their Clanmates' vigil. It would last all night, and then what? ShadowClan still had no leader. The cats were silent, moving slowly as if their limbs had frozen, none quite meeting another's eye. *The blood of these cats stains all our paws.*

Flowerstem alone seemed to have her voice; she wove among the stunned cats, comforting them, sending them to the fresh-kill pile to eat: "We have to keep up our strength. There is still sickness in the air; no more cats must die." Quietly she asked two of the senior warriors to take out hunting patrols with all the apprentices. "There is no need for them to spend all day looking at these fallen warriors. Keep them busy, but battle training would not be appropriate, I think." Her Clanmates nodded and led the younger cats silently out of the clearing.

Then Flowerstem approached Redscar. Her eyes looked dull with shock, but she spoke calmly. "Is there anything I can do for

CODE
9

you, Redscar? Fetch herbs or water?"

Redscar shook his head. There was nothing any cat could do. "I'll be in my den," he told her and headed for the thicket of hawthorn that screened his nest and his store of herbs. He stumbled into his nest, feeling many seasons older than he had when he last lay down, and closed his eyes.

"Redscar? Redscar, wake up."

He opened his eyes. He was lying in a clearing among beech trees, their branches black and sharp against the snow-colored sky. The grass beneath him was crisp and cold; he jumped up, shivering.

"Redscar, you must find a new leader for ShadowClan."

"Snowstar?"

The gray cat nodded. "I have been watching my Clan, and I grieve for every one of my cats. Most of all, for Brightwhisker, who would have been a great leader, and for Jumpfoot and Mossfire who let ambition cloud their senses and sharpen their claws. You must put this right, my friend."

"What can I do?" Redscar wailed.

"You will choose a new leader," Snowstar meowed. "And that cat must choose a deputy at once. A Clan must never be left like this again, a headless creature that wades into blood because it cannot see. At the next Gathering, the new leader must introduce a new rule for the warrior code: Deputies must be replaced by moonhigh, so a leader will never be alone for more than half a day. Now tell me, who would you choose as your next leader?"

Redscar started to protest that he couldn't, wouldn't, choose, but the look in Snowstar's eyes silenced him. "Flowerstem," he meowed. "She watched her sister die in front of her, but her only thoughts were to make the Clan feel safe and keep them occupied before tonight's vigil."

"A wise choice. So tell the Clan."

Redscar stared at him. "Why should they listen to me? I've done nothing for them, nothing."

Snowstar narrowed his eyes. "You're their medicine cat. They will listen to you, if you use the right words." The beech trees were looking paler now, blurring against the white clouds. Snowstar was fading, too. "Go now, Redscar," he called. "Appoint Flowerstem as the new leader of ShadowClan!"

Redscar blinked and he was back in his nest with a crow feather tickling his ear. He shook his head irritably. The Clan was in turmoil. They must think their warrior ancestors had given up on them.

No words, but maybe an action?

He padded into the clearing. The camp was quiet and deserted, apart from the bodies of Mossfire and Jumpfoot lying in the shelter of some dry bracken. He slipped out of the camp and trotted to a place where an oak tree grew on ground that was less marshy than the rest of the territory. Mossfire and Jumpfoot would be buried near here. At the foot of the tree, sheltered from the wind, grew a bunch of delicate white flowers, the color of snow and the shape of raindrops.

CODE
9

Checking there were no cats around, he nipped one of the snowdrops off at the base of its stalk. Laying it on the ground, he pulled off the smooth white petals, leaving just the stem. Then he curled it up and pushed it into a clump of moss that he dug up from underneath a tree root. Picking up the moss in his teeth, he headed back for the camp. No cat would question a medicine cat fetching moss; it was used for bedding as well as to carry water.

When he returned to the camp, there were more cats around. The hunting patrols had come back with a fair haul of fresh-kill, and pale sunlight had tempted their Clanmates out to eat. Redscar nodded to one or two as he crossed the clearing. As he passed the fallen log used by the leaders to address the Clan, he relaxed his grip on the moss and felt the snowdrop stalk spring out. Quick as lightning, he dropped the moss and kicked it with his paw so that it rolled underneath a hawthorn, out of sight.

"Look!" he cried, gazing down at the pale green stem lying at his paws. It was as slim as a whisker, still quivering from where it had uncurled. "Did any cat bring this into the camp?"

His Clanmates gathered around. "It's a snowdrop stalk. They only grow by the oak tree, right?" meowed one of the apprentices.

Redscar lifted his head and faced them. His paws were shaking but he sank his claws into the earth to keep them still. "It's a sign from StarClan," he announced. "They want us to know their choice for the new ShadowClan leader."

"Who?" gasped a she-cat plump with kits.

Redscar touched the stalk with his paw. "Flowerstem."

There was a gasp, then murmurs of agreement.

The ginger-and-white she-cat was pushed to the front of the cats. She looked dazed. "I don't know what to say," she began.

"Just say you will lead us, as StarClan wishes," meowed Redscar.

Flowerstem looked down at the snowdrop stalk, then over her shoulder at her motionless sister. "To honor Mossfire's memory and Jumpfoot's, yes, I will." She dipped her head as joyful yowls rose around her.

Maybe StarClan had needed Redscar's help to send this sign, but it was what Snowstar wanted. And he would tell Flowerstar to choose her deputy before the moon reached its height, in front of the bodies of her fallen Clanmates, and Brightwhisker, so that their spirits could hear and approve her choice.

"Thank you, Snowstar," he whispered.

CODE TEN

A GATHERING OF ALL CLANS IS HELD AT
THE FULL MOON DURING A TRUCE THAT LASTS
FOR THE NIGHT. THERE SHALL BE NO FIGHTING
AMONG CLANS AT THIS TIME.

*Even though the Gatherings started with the very
beginning of the warrior code, the full-moon truce did not become
part of the code until much later. Now the truce is respected
by every cat, whether it is because they value the chance
to exchange news in peace with their close neighbors, or because
they are afraid of what their warrior ancestors might do if they
break the code. Come with me to Fourtrees long ago,
when the ancestors first looked down on the full-moon gathering
and bound the Clan cats to the full-moon truce.*

The Vanishing Moon

The four giant oaks cast thick shadows across the moon-washed clearing as Finchstar crouched at the top of the slope. Behind him, his Clanmates waited, the air clouded with their breath. Several cats dotted the hollow already, circling to keep warm as they exchanged cautious greetings with warriors from rival Clans.

"Come on, ThunderClan!" Finchstar called. He stood up and began to run down the slope, stretching his tail up so his Clanmates could follow.

"Good," muttered Daisyheart, his deputy, as she bounded beside him. "If I'd stayed still much longer I'd have turned into an icicle."

Frost crackled under Finchstar's paws as he jumped onto the flat stretch of grass. Two WindClan elders nodded to him and a RiverClan warrior called a greeting as he wove his way through the cats to the Great Rock.

"How's the prey running, Finchstar?" SkyClan's leader, Hawkstar, asked as he leaped onto the top of the smooth silver boulder.

"Fast," he replied. "It doesn't like being out in this weather any more than we do!"

"Our rabbits run so quickly, they're nothing but muscle and bone when we catch them," Dovestar, the WindClan leader, put in. "So tough to chew!"

The RiverClan leader, Reedstar, said nothing. He was sitting on the far side of the rock, as far from Hawkstar as he could get without falling off. Their Clans had been at war over a strip of shoreline for almost three seasons; one battle had led to the death of SkyClan's former leader, Dewstar, and his Clanmates were far from forgiving their rivals across the water.

Finchstar looked down at the clearing. "ShadowClan not here yet? It's not like Ripplestar to be late."

Dovestar lifted his haunches off the stone and settled down again with his tail curled up. "I'll stick to this rock if we don't start soon. It's colder than ice."

Reedstar shifted, sending his shadow flickering over the

edge of the boulder, crisp in the moonlight. "Maybe the frost has delayed them?"

The tip of Hawkstar's tail twitched. "Something's wrong," he murmured. "My pelt's been itching all day."

"Fleas," muttered Reedstar.

Finchstar glared at him. It was full moon, the one night they were supposed to put their rivalry aside and share news for the good of all the Clans.

There was a hiss like wind at the edge of the clearing. Finchstar pricked his ears and stared into the moon shadows. Was that a branch waving in the breeze, or something more?

Why does Fourtrees suddenly feel unsafe?

"ShadowClan! Attack!"

The shadows exploded, spitting and yowling. The cats in the clearing whirled to face them, but before they could brace themselves, ShadowClan warriors fell on them, claws and fangs bared. Within a heartbeat, the hollow thrashed and rippled like a river full of salmon. The leaders of the Clans stood on the edge of Great Rock, staring down in horror. Then Reedstar leaped down, quickly followed by Hawkstar and Dovestar. Finchstar heard them screech orders to their senior warriors, splitting them into battle groups to defend the elders and apprentices who had come to the Gathering.

A ginger-and-white face flashed up at Finchstar from the turmoil at the foot of the rock.

"Help us, Finchstar!" Daisyheart wailed, before she whipped around to claw a ShadowClan warrior over his ears.

Finchstar bunched his haunches, ready to jump down, when a shadow fell across him. He looked up. Ripplestar stood beside him on the Great Rock, his yellow eyes glowing as they watched the battle.

"I bet you never thought I'd do it," he meowed, so quietly Finchstar could hardly hear him over the screeches and yowls from below.

"Do what? Attack four Clans when they came in peace to a Gathering, with elders among them?" Finchstar hissed. "No, Ripplestar. I never thought you'd be as cowardly as that."

The black-and-orange cat lashed his tail. "Hardly the actions of a coward, to take on all four Clans at once!"

Slipping his claws free, Finchstar sprang at Ripplestar, bringing him down on top of the rock with a muffled thud. The ShadowClan leader squirmed around until he was lying on his back, then raked Finchstar's belly with his hind paws. Finchstar sank his claws deeper into the loose fur around Ripplestar's neck, feeling the slender bones underneath.

"Call off your cats!" he spat. "This attack is wrong!"

Ripplestar scrabbled to his feet and glared at Finchstar. "I wouldn't call an easy victory wrong," he gloated. "Look at your precious cats now."

Finchstar risked a sideways look. The battle was slowing; many cats were slumped on the silver grass, bleeding and motionless. ShadowClan warriors paced among them, ready to lash out if any cat stirred.

"No!" Finchstar yowled. "You can't do this!"

He jumped at Ripplestar but his hind paws skidded on the icy rock, and the ShadowClan leader stepped easily out of the way.

"So you keep telling me," Ripplestar observed. "But I seem to have done it anyway! Looks like I don't have to listen to you, Finchstar."

For a heartbeat, the hollow glowed bright white, outlining every leaf, every blade of grass, every whisker. Then the air cracked, and the two cats on the rock flung themselves down, clinging to the stone as it trembled beneath them. Finchstar pressed his face into the cold surface and waited for the roll of thunder to fade away. A storm in leaf-bare? But there were no clouds. The moon was out. . . .

"Finchstar!" His name was barely a whisper, drowned by another clap of thunder slamming into the forest.

Finchstar forced himself to lift his head. His eyes were still dazzled by the first flash of lightning and he had to blink to see clearly. The clearing was much darker than before, so dark he couldn't see Ripplestar. The moon had vanished. The sky was covered with thick black clouds.

Finchstar shook his head, waiting for his eyes to adjust. He could make out the trees now and the shape of the Great Rock beneath him. But still no Ripplestar.

"Help . . . me. . . ."

A scratching sound came from the edge of the rock. Finchstar saw Ripplestar's yellow eyes staring over the top and his black-and-orange paws.

"Hold on!" Finchstar yowled. He hurled himself across the stone, reaching out with his front paws to grab Ripplestar's scruff and haul him to safety.

CODE 10

He was a mouse-length away when the sky burst open again, filling the air with blazing white light and letting out a roar that sounded like every tree in the forest was falling at once. Finchstar crashed down onto the rock and pressed his paws into his ears, trying to block the explosion of noise that bounced around the hollow. He heard a thin, terrified wail as Ripplestar lost his grip and plunged to the ground.

The clearing was silent. The cats still on their paws were staring at something Finchstar couldn't see, at the foot of Great Rock. Then a heavily scarred gray warrior rushed forward.

"Ripplestar! No!"

Finchstar bowed his head. The ShadowClan leader must have been on his ninth life. He was young to die as a leader, but perhaps his battle-hungry career had used up the rest of his lives too quickly.

"Murderer!"

The gray warrior—Marshscar, the ShadowClan deputy, Finchstar suddenly realized—was glaring up at him.

"Come down here and let me avenge our leader's death!" Marshscar snarled.

"I didn't kill Ripplestar!" Finchstar told him, feeling the fur rise along his spine.

"Then who did?" the gray cat challenged.

Finchstar looked up at the bubbling clouds that hid the full moon. The truce had been broken the moment Ripplestar told his warriors to attack the unsuspecting Clans. Then the moon disappeared and a storm came, bringing thunder and lightning that shook the forest to its roots.

"StarClan killed him," Finchstar announced. His paws trembled. Would his warrior ancestors forgive him for accusing them of cold-blooded murder? But the sky stayed quiet.

"StarClan has punished ShadowClan for breaking the truce and attacking on the night of a full moon," Finchstar went on. "There is no clearer message they could send."

A pale brown tabby from RiverClan stepped forward. "StarClan, forgive us all for fighting!" he yowled.

"From now on, the full moon will be honored by every Clan!" Dovestar called.

Finchstar stepped to the edge of the rock and raised his voice so every cat could hear him. There would be time afterward to tend to the wounded and carry them home. For now, he had to make sure this would never happen again.

"There will be a new rule in the warrior code!" he declared. "There will be no fighting at the time of the new moon. The truce is sacred and will be protected for every Gathering."

StarClan, forgive us.

CODE ELEVEN

> ## BOUNDARIES MUST BE CHECKED
> ## AND MARKED DAILY. CHALLENGE ALL
> ## TRESPASSING CATS.

*Not all parts of the warrior code come from
tragedy and conflict. Some, like this one, were needed to
clear up a long-running misunderstanding and avoid
the need for blood to be spilled.*

Poppycloud's Rule

The air was so still, Poppycloud could hear herself breathing. She waited with one paw raised, knowing the dried leaves would crackle loud as thunder as soon as she set it down. It was leaf-fall, and in SkyClan, with all its trees and little undergrowth, moving silently was almost impossible. The hair along her spine prickled as she strained to listen.

"Can you hear anything, Poppycloud? Can you, can you?"

Bracken rustled behind her and she turned, resigned, as a small black-and-white cat exploded from the brittle stems.

"Yes, Mottlepaw, I can hear something," she meowed.

The apprentice stopped dead and stared at her. "Really? What?"

CODE TEN

"*You!*"

Mottlepaw's tail drooped. "But I tried to be quiet, like you showed me."

Poppycloud walked over to him and touched the tip of his ear with her nose. "I think we need to practice some more."

Mottlepaw wriggled free and padded up to the border. "Why does Rowanstar make us come this way when he knows ThunderClan doesn't like it?"

Poppycloud shrugged and nudged a piece of leaf off her tortoiseshell fur. "I think he likes to know if anything happens in our territory. If we just stuck to the best hunting areas, we'd never visit some places."

"Like this one." Mottlepaw's voice was muffled as he stuck his head into a clump of long grass. "I can't smell any birds *anywhere!*"

"That's because you're in ThunderClan territory!" came a snarl.

Poppycloud spun around. A broad-shouldered brown tom stood a fox-length away, his lip curled to reveal sharp yellow teeth.

"What a surprise!" he hissed. "SkyClan cats lurking on the border again. What's wrong with your own territory?"

Poppycloud felt her hackles raise. "Nothing!" she retorted. "We have every right to go anywhere inside our borders."

"Which your apprentice isn't," the ThunderClan warrior growled.

CODE
11

Mottlepaw pulled back from the clump of grass and stood with his head down, trembling.

"Mottlepaw, come over here," Poppycloud ordered. The black-and-white apprentice shot toward her, swerving around the ThunderClan tom, who hissed as he went past.

"It was a mistake," Poppycloud pointed out. "We weren't trying to steal your prey."

Ferns parted and another cat joined the brown warrior. She fixed her startlingly green gaze on Poppycloud. "Why are there always SkyClan cats snooping around here? Is your own Clan so bad that you want to join ours?"

"Never!" Poppycloud retorted. "We prefer not to chew through mouthfuls of fur when we're eating our prey!"

The brown tom tipped his head to one side. "Oh, and feathers are so much tastier, are they?"

"Come on, Oatwhisker," urged the she-cat. "We're wasting our time. If these dumb cats want to spy on us, they won't learn much from the bushes around here. I don't think I've even been to this part of the territory before."

Oatwhisker narrowed his eyes at Poppycloud. "Don't think this is over. I'm going to tell Lionstar I caught SkyClan cats hanging around the border yet again, and I wouldn't want to be in your pelts if he thinks you're planning an attack."

He stalked out of the clearing with his green-eyed Clanmate. As soon as they had vanished, Poppycloud turned to Mottlepaw. "How many times do I have to tell you? You can't go into another Clan's territory!"

Mottlepaw sniffed. "I wasn't doing anything wrong," he complained. "Anyway, it's so hard to tell where our territory turns into ThunderClan's. It's not like there's a river in the way!"

Poppycloud opened her jaws to taste the air. Mottlepaw was

right: The scents of the different Clans were very faint here, so she couldn't blame her apprentice for straying too far. "Come on," she meowed. "We'd better go and tell Rowanstar what happened, in case ThunderClan makes a fuss."

"He won't be angry with me, will he?" Mottlepaw whimpered. "I already had to put mouse bile on the elders' ticks after I scared Morningmist's kits with my tiger roar."

"I'll tell him it was an honest mistake," Poppycloud promised. "Just try not to get into any more trouble on the way back."

"Tell Rowanstar that we wish to speak with him."

A buzz of curiosity ran through the camp.

"Who's that?"

"ThunderClan cats!"

"What do they want?"

"Have they come to get me?"

Poppycloud looked down at Mottlepaw, who was staring at her with his blue eyes stretched wide. "I'm sure they haven't come to get you," she meowed. "But I'm glad we told Rowanstar what happened on the border."

Oddfoot, a brown tabby who was born with one of his paws twisted inward, led the visitors into the clearing. A massive tom with long ginger hair padded beside him, flanked by the green-eyed gray tabby Poppycloud had met on the border and a dark brown tom who looked as if he expected to be jumped on at any moment. Poppycloud drew in her breath sharply: This must be serious if Lionstar had come himself.

Nightmask, the SkyClan deputy, met them in the center of the camp. "Lionstar, Greeneyes," he greeted them with a nod of his head. Poppycloud stared at the gray tabby with new interest; she hadn't realized this was the recently appointed ThunderClan deputy.

"You are, of course, welcome to speak with Rowanstar. Will he know what this is about?"

Greeneyes curled her lip. "It's about your warriors spying on us!" she hissed.

Lionstar flicked his tail, warning her to stay quiet. "I am concerned that there are always SkyClan cats on the edge of our territory, and I want to know what they're doing there."

"I think you'll find they're on the edge of our territory," came a deep voice. Rowanstar, his black-and-brown coat gleaming in the weak sunlight, padded out of his den. "So there shouldn't be any problem."

"But there's nothing there!" Lionstar argued. "Nothing but the start of ThunderClan's territory."

Rowanstar glanced at Poppycloud. "From what I hear, it's not always easy to tell where your territory begins. Perhaps if you visited your border more often, your scent would be clearer."

Lionstar's hackles raised, swelling him to nearly twice his size. Mottlepaw shrank behind Poppycloud with a whimper.

"ThunderClan should not have to patrol its boundaries to make sure SkyClan isn't trespassing!" Lionstar growled.

"If you patrolled more often, there would be less danger of us crossing the border!" Rowanstar flashed back.

Greeneyes stepped forward. "The warrior code says nothing about it being a Clan's responsibility to keep cats out! It should be obvious that other Clans aren't allowed across the border."

"Well, maybe the code should say something!"

All eyes turned on Poppycloud. She snapped her mouth shut, feeling as if her pelt were on fire. *Did I really just say that in front of the leaders of two Clans?*

"Yay! Go, Poppycloud!" Mottlepaw cheered behind her.

Poppycloud silenced him with a glare.

Rowanstar put his head to one side. "That's an interesting theory, Poppycloud. Go on."

Poppycloud felt a small nose nudge her from behind. She shot a fierce glance at her apprentice before padding into the clearing. Every cat watched her. Greeneyes looked scornful; this made Poppycloud square her shoulders and tilt her chin defiantly toward the ThunderClan deputy.

"I . . . I just think all the quarreling about SkyClan being on the ThunderClan border would be cleared up if every Clan did the same as Rowanstar wants us to do: have regular patrols around the entire territory. That way, the scents of each Clan would be left behind more frequently, not just in the places where the cats hunt most often, and boundaries would be more clearly marked. Any cats that crossed over the border could be punished, because it wouldn't be a mistake."

Rowanstar nodded. "And if both ThunderClan and SkyClan patrols regularly went along our shared border, then neither Clan could be accused of spying or trying to trespass." He flicked his tail at Poppycloud. "That's a great idea."

CODE
11

Lionstar hissed. "So you think the warrior code should tell us how to defend our territories, do you? What kind of leader would be mouse-brained enough to need instructions like that?"

"The kind of leader who thinks that a patrol walking along their own boundaries is planning an attack," Rowanstar meowed smoothly.

"Well, I think it's a ridiculous idea," sniffed Greeneyes. "The

Clans have lived in these territories for more moons than any cat can remember, and we've never needed the warrior code to tell us how to protect our borders. Clearly some cats are more mouse-brained than others."

Slanting her eyes at Poppycloud, she turned away with a huff.

Lionstar started to turn and follow his deputy, but Rowanstar called out, "Wait!" When Lionstar faced him again, the SkyClan leader announced, "I shall put forward Poppycloud's idea at the next Gathering. We should let the other leaders decide—not because I think any Clan cat needs to be reminded that their territories should be well defended, but because it will stop needless suspicion over border patrols."

Lionstar stretched one forepaw and let his claws slide out. "You do realize that if the other leaders agree to this ridiculous rule, then I'll be allowed to tear the fur off any of your apprentices who just happen to cross our border?"

From the corner of her eye, Poppycloud saw Mottlepaw back into the brambles that surrounded the apprentices' den, until only his white patches could be seen.

Rowanstar didn't flinch. "And we'd punish any ThunderClan cats who trespassed," he meowed. "The situation will be clear and fair—like the boundaries."

Lionstar spun around and started to stalk toward the entrance. "Until the next Gathering, Rowanstar. We'll see what the other Clans think of your idea then."

"Indeed we will," Rowanstar murmured as the ThunderClan cats were swallowed up by the bracken.

Poppycloud watched until the fronds of bracken stopped trembling. *If this becomes part of the warrior code, I will live forever!* She shook her head to chase away such huge dreams and looked for Mottlepaw. Adding rules to the warrior code was kit's play compared with trying to keep her apprentice in line. But he was a quick learner and would one day make a warrior to be proud of.

Not that I could be any prouder of him than I am already, as his mother as well as his mentor. With a soft purr of amusement, she went in search of her unruly son.

Who Goes There? Whitestorm Teaches Border Tactics

Once the borders were fixed, cats of neighboring Clans started to meet frequently across their borders when on patrol. It became apparent that cats of all Clans must know how to handle disputes. Here's Whitestorm training a group of ThunderClan apprentices in border tactics.

Is every cat here? Firepaw, Graypaw, Ravenpaw, Sandpaw, and Dustpaw? Dustpaw, stop trying to push Firepaw into the brambles. I'm not blind; I can see what you're doing. Firepaw, go to the other end of the line. Sandpaw, he does *not* have fleas! Stand still, all of you.

CODE 11

As Lionheart told you, we're going to practice border defense today. You can be the patrol, and I'll be a deputy from another Clan who's crossed the boundary. Who'd like to lead the patrol? Don't look so terrified, Ravenpaw. I won't make you be the leader if you don't want to be. Graypaw, why don't you have first turn? If you could just pick up that stick in your mouth and use it to draw a line across the sand, we'll call that the border. Sandpaw, it doesn't matter that the line is wobbly. Boundaries aren't whisker-straight,

are they? So, you're on
that side, walking along
on a dawn patrol. Off
you go, patrol!

Did you really
need to yawn like
that, Graypaw? Oh, I
see, it's because it's the
dawn patrol, and you're
tired. Well, let's pretend
you all had a really good night's
sleep and are full of energy. Now, what should you be doing?
Yes, sniffing, tasting the air—what for? That's right, Sandpaw.
ThunderClan border marks. And what else? Yes, Firepaw. The
border marks of the other Clan. But only where the two borders
meet. Beside the river and the Thunderpath, it would be bad news
to find any scents of RiverClan or ShadowClan, because it would
mean they'd crossed over from their side. So keep sniffing.

Maybe not that much, Sandpaw. Have a good sneeze and you
should get the sand out of your nose. So, border marks, border
marks. Can you smell both sets? Good. But what's this? A cat
from another Clan has ignored the marks and stepped over your
border?

No, Ravenpaw, I didn't mean we were actually being invaded.
The cat from the other Clan is me. See how I just stepped over
the line in the sand? What are you going to do about it? Wha . . .
whoa! Stop treading on my ears!

Well, yes, Dustpaw, launching an attack and knocking me
back across the border is one option. But is it wise to take on a cat
twice your size? Or a trained warrior with more experience than
you? The purpose of a patrol is to assess the situation and report

back to your Clan leader. You won't be able to do that if your pelt is clawed to shreds at the farthest part of the territory from the camp. Any other ideas?

How about asking what I'm doing? I might have a valid reason for crossing the border, especially if I'm alone. That's right, Graystripe: *What do you want?* is a good way to start. Don't be too hostile: Remember, you are in the stronger position, because this is your territory and you have the right to defend it. Unless I have a very good explanation for crossing your border, I don't have any rights at all. What do you think my reply might be?

Yes, Ravenpaw, I might need your help. My Clan might have been invaded, we might have serious trouble with prey, or we might have sickness that needs your herbs. All these reasons would mean that I am *weak*, so you can allow me into your territory but never out of sight.

If I am hostile, then meet me with hostility—which isn't the same as aggression, Dustpaw. You've started with a strong challenge—What do you want?—and now you need to give me some sort of warning. Ravenpaw, what would you say?

Hmmm. If you're going to threaten to claw a cat's ears, you should try not to look so terrified at the prospect. Firepaw, would you like to try? Ah, yes, I like that you indicated the rest of your patrol. It's always good to let the enemy know they're outnumbered. Sandpaw, *put that fire ant down*. No, I don't care that Firepaw might not know what it is. Now is not the right time to show him—and he certainly doesn't need to get bitten by one.

So, you've challenged the trespasser, warned me that there's a whole patrol here that can take me to your Clan leader if that's what I wish; what next? That's right, Graypaw, let me—the intruder—speak. If I can't give you a convincing explanation for what I'm doing on your territory, if I don't ask to be taken to

CODE
11

Bluestar at once, then chase me off with no more questions. Don't provoke a full-scale war—chasing means chasing, not catching and clawing. Just make it clear that you will defend your boundaries from any kind of invasion, even one paw across the border. A good warrior is always ready to fight, but only if it's absolutely necessary: A good warrior will seek a peaceful, claws-sheathed solution first.

You will all make good warriors one day. Don't look so doubtful, Ravenpaw. You need to find only a little more courage to be as good as your denmates. Your hunting skills are excellent—Dustpaw, you'd do well to watch him. Who knows? You might even lead this Clan one day!

Now, back to camp, all of you, and leave this old warrior to enjoy the sun in peace.

CODE TWELVE

> ## NO WARRIOR MAY NEGLECT A KIT
> ## IN PAIN OR IN DANGER, EVEN IF THAT KIT
> ## IS FROM A DIFFERENT CLAN.

*The strength of a Clan does not depend only on
the strength of its warriors. We also need to raise healthy kits to
follow in the paw steps of their Clanmates. For this reason,
kits are protected by all the cats in the forest, wherever their Clan
loyalties lie. But it was not always so. As you will see, it sometimes
takes a tragedy to teach the simplest of lessons.*

A Loss for All Clans

Graywing stood on the flattened rock overlooking the river
and closed her eyes, letting the fine mist spray her face.
Heavy newleaf rains had swollen the water to a fast black torrent
that spat and tumbled out of the gorge. Today the rain had stopped,
sending Graywing and most of the RiverClan cats out of the camp
to stretch their cramped legs and see which parts of the territory
were underwater.

"Don't fall in!" warned a voice behind Graywing. "All this
damp weather is bound to bring coughs and stiff joints, so we
need our medicine cat!"

Graywing turned to see a sleek tortoiseshell she-cat padding over the stones toward her. "Don't worry, Brindleclaw. I have no intention of going for a swim today."

A ginger tom slid out of the reeds behind Brindleclaw. He scowled at the flooded river. "We'll be living off voles for a while," he predicted. "We can't risk any of our warriors trying to catch fish in that."

Brindleclaw nodded. "I'll warn the hunting patrols to stay well clear of the river until the level has gone down. Perhaps you could take a patrol into the fields, Foxwhisker?"

The ginger warrior grunted in agreement.

Graywing jumped down from the rock. "I need to see if my supply of mallow has survived the floods. I'll see you back at the camp."

Brindleclaw opened her mouth to reply, then stopped, staring straight past Graywing with a look of horror in her eyes. Graywing spun around. Three tiny fluffy shapes were clinging to the side of the gorge on the WindClan side, their hind legs dangling over the foaming water below.

"Great StarClan!" snarled Foxwhisker. "What on earth do those kits think they're doing?"

Brindleclaw was already running along the bank toward the mouth of the gorge. "It doesn't matter what they're doing!" she called over her shoulder. "They're going to fall!"

As she spoke, one of the kits lost its grip on the rocks and fell like a ripe apple into the river. There was a high-pitched squeal from one of its denmates, and another bundle plunged down into the water. Graywing felt as if her paws were frozen to the ground; the only thing she could do was watch as the third kit fell. It was impossible to see where they landed; any little splashes were swallowed up in the foam as the river burst out of the narrow canyon.

"Come on!" Brindleclaw yowled. "We have to help them!" She reached the end of the open river and raced down the shore to where the water exploded out of the gorge.

"Stop!" Graywing screeched. Her paws suddenly let go of their grip on the stones and she tore after Brindleclaw with Foxwhisker on her heels. "You can't go in!"

Brindleclaw stared at her. "What do you mean? Those kits will drown if we don't get them out!"

Graywing felt a pain in her chest as if she had just swallowed a boulder. "They're probably dead already," she forced herself to say. "We can't risk our own lives trying to save them. Besides, they are WindClan kits. They are not ours to save."

Beside them, there was a tiny squeak from the waves, and a paw the size of a blackberry shot above the surface before disappearing again.

"They're not dead!" Brindleclaw gasped. She bunched her haunches, ready to leap into the water, but Graywing took hold of her scruff with her teeth.

"I can't let you do this!" she choked through thick tortoiseshell fur. "StarClan made me medicine cat to serve RiverClan, not risk my Clanmates' lives to help other Clans."

Brindleclaw wrenched herself free and glared at Graywing. "How can you watch those kits drown without doing anything? What kind of a medicine cat are you?"

"One that is loyal to her Clan above all else," Graywing murmured. The pain in her chest swelled until she couldn't breathe, and her vision blurred.

"Graywing is right," meowed Foxwhisker. "It would have been madness to risk the life of a RiverClan warrior to save cats from another Clan. Come on, Brindleclaw."

The two warriors crunched away over the stones. Graywing

CODE
12

let her legs crumple beneath her until she was slumped on the pebbles, feeling them hard and cold through her pelt. The only thing she could think of was the pitiful cry from the river as the kit had been swept away.

Ivystar, the RiverClan leader, was shocked to hear about the WindClan kits, but agreed that Graywing had been right not to let Brindleclaw jump in. She studied her medicine cat closely as Graywing stood before her with her head bowed. "It wasn't your fault those kits fell in," Ivystar murmured. "I'm sure they were told over and over to stay away from the gorge."

Graywing shook her head. "Their poor mother. Such a terrible loss for their Clan."

"And it could have been a terrible loss for RiverClan, too, if Brindleclaw had gone in after them," Ivystar pointed out. "Now go get some rest. I'll tell the patrols to keep an eye out for your mallow plants."

Graywing walked slowly to her den. Two RiverClan kits, Wildkit and Minnowkit, bounced around her.

"Did you really see those kits drown?"

"Were they all wet and horrid looking?"

"Did their eyes fall out?"

"Wildkit! Minnowkit! Stop asking such horrible questions!" their mother scolded from the nursery. "Come back here at once!"

Graywing didn't look up. She padded to her nest and curled up with her nose under her tail. *It's not my fault that those kits died.*

So why do I feel so guilty?

When Graywing opened her eyes, moonlight flooded her den and the camp was still and quiet. She sat up, shocked that she'd slept for so long. The reeds that shielded her den rattled, and she heard a soft murmur from the clearing. Wondering if a cat had been taken ill, Graywing slipped out of her nest and pushed her way through the reeds. Three cats stood in the center of the camp, their fur frosted by the dazzling white light.

"Who are you?" Graywing stammered. These weren't RiverClan warriors, and she didn't recognize them from Gatherings. She wondered how they had managed to get all the way into the camp without being challenged.

The tallest of the strangers, hard-muscled beneath his brown tabby coat, dipped his head. "Greetings, Graywing," he meowed. "My name is Runningstorm of WindClan. This is Wolfheart"— he nodded to the elegant gray she-cat beside him—"and our leader, Smallstar."

The third cat, whose tiny frame was covered in sleek black-and-white fur, looked at Graywing. His blue eyes were friendly as he mewed, "We have traveled far to see you."

Graywing looked from one cat to the other. "I don't understand. Has something happened to Fallowstar?"

Smallstar shook his head. "Fallowstar is fine. We are the cats who would have been."

Graywing stared at them in horror. The image of three terrified bundles, falling one by one into the churning river, filled her eyes. "You are the kits who drowned," she whispered.

Wolfheart bent her head. "That is so. Come, we have something to show you."

She turned and led the way across the clearing toward the nursery. Graywing followed without having to tell her paws what to do; they seemed to be carrying her on their own.

Runningstorm nosed aside the bramble that was draped across the entrance to the nursery, protecting the precious cats inside. "Look," he urged Graywing.

Oh, StarClan, let our kits be all right, Graywing prayed as she poked her head inside. *Had the WindClan kits returned to punish her by hurting the youngest RiverClan cats?*

The den smelled warm and milky, and enough moonlight filtered through the branches for Graywing to see Hayberry curled around Wildkit and Minnowkit, who snuffled gently in their sleep. Hayberry's flank rose and fell in time with her kits' breathing, and although her eyelids flickered when Graywing looked at her, she didn't stir.

Graywing pulled her head out. "They're safe," she breathed.

Smallstar looked surprised. "Of course. Did you think we'd hurt one hair on their pelts? Kits are the most special part of a Clan. They are the warriors who will defend their Clanmates in moons to come, the hunters who will find food even in the coldest leaf-bare, the cats who will have kits of their own to pass on everything they have learned. A Clan that has no kits might as well be dead."

"And if one Clan dies, the survival of all the Clans is threatened," Runningstorm added. "We may be rivals, but we are linked by StarClan, stronger than rock, stronger than tree roots, stronger than the water in the river."

"I'm sorry." Graywing faced the shining warriors and bowed her head. "I should have let Brindleclaw try to save you. WindClan's loss is ours, too."

There was no reply. She lifted her head to see the three cats fading away, returning to their home in the stars.

Graywing blinked. She was lying in her nest, the moss and feathers underneath her looking as if a battle had been fought there the night before. Graywing hauled herself up and stretched one hind leg at a time. Why did she feel as if she hadn't slept at all?

The dream!

She raced out of the den and went straight to Ivystar. "I have to take a patrol out," she panted.

Ivystar put her head to one side. "Do we need herbs so desperately? Has a cat fallen ill?"

"No, nothing like that. Please, let me take Brindleclaw and Foxwhisker. I'll explain everything later."

"Very well. But be careful. The river will still be flooded."

Graywing shot out of Ivystar's den and went to wake up Brindleclaw and Foxwhisker. The she-cat was still icy cold toward her, but Graywing didn't try to apologize or even tell the warriors what they were doing. They would understand soon enough. . . .

Graywing led them along the shore heading downriver, toward Sunningrocks. She slowed as they drew near the looming gray shapes and started to sniff carefully along the river's edge.

"Are you looking for something?" Foxwhisker asked.

Graywing looked up. "I want to find the kits who drowned yesterday," she mewed. "They should have lived to become warriors for their Clan. We need to take them back home."

Brindleclaw stared at her in shock. "But yesterday you said we couldn't have anything to do with them because they weren't RiverClan!"

Graywing nodded. "And I was wrong. Kits should be precious to all Clans. After we have taken these three back to WindClan, I will ask Ivystar to suggest an addition to the warrior code: that kits should be protected by every cat in the forest, regardless of which Clan they come from. All our futures depend on them."

"Over there," came a quiet meow. Foxwhisker was standing on the edge of the water, facing away from them. He jerked his muzzle toward the far bank, where a tangle of sodden fur had

CODE
12

been washed up against a branch.

"Come on," murmured Graywing. She and her Clanmates slipped into the water and paddled strongly through the current toward the branch. The swollen river tried to drag them away, and battered them with twigs and other debris washed down from the gorge, but they stretched their necks to keep their muzzles above the surface and churned with legs well used to swimming. Graywing reached the kits first. Through the filthy, water-dark fur, she could just make out patches of black and white in the shape nearest to her. It was Smallkit, who would have been leader of his Clan had he survived. Graywing picked him up and carried him back to the RiverClan shore. Foxwhisker followed with Runningkit, and Brindleclaw brought Wolfkit.

They laid their tiny burdens on the shore to get their breath back. Graywing touched each body with her muzzle. "Your Clan will honor you with a burial for the warriors that you would have been," she told them. "And you will live on in the law that makes every Clan responsible for the safety of kits, wherever they are born.

"Precious kits, walk safely among the stars."

A Kit in Trouble

No cat doubts that cats of all Clans must protect kits. But we know from bitter experience that not all kits grow up to honor the warrior code that once protected them. Every full-grown tyrant or murderer was once a tiny bundle of fluff that swelled a mother's heart with pride. If we could see into the future, would we protect each and every kit the same?

Brackenfoot curled his lip as he pushed through the broad, sticky plants that grew along the Thunderpath that bordered ShadowClan's territory. He didn't share his Clanmates' taste for monster-kill, and the stench and the noise coming from the strip of black stone made him blind and deaf to everything else. He waited for the roar of the monsters to fade, then bounded onto the narrow strip of foul-smelling grass.

Archeye was sniffing at some crumpled gray and white feathers lying on the edge of the Thunderpath. "Looks like we might be able to take some pigeon home," he commented.

It won't taste of pigeon, thought Brackenfoot. *It'll taste burned and bitter, like licking a monster's paw.*

To his relief, Hollyflower wrinkled her nose. "There's not enough meat left to bother with," she told Archeye.

The still, hot air was ruffled by the sound of a growl; Brackenfoot spun around, expecting to see a curious dog that had broken away from its Twoleg. But nothing stirred on ShadowClan's hunting grounds. Then Hollyflower yowled, "Fox!"

Brackenfoot stiffened. A red-brown creature with the familiar pointed snout was standing among the ferns on the far side of the Thunderpath, in ThunderClan's territory. The fox's fur bristled

along its back, and it held its head low.

"Is it stalking us?" Archeye whispered.

"Foxes don't hunt full-grown cats," Crowclaw whispered back. "Not unless they're starving."

Brackenfoot peered closer. There was something trembling on the very edge of the Thunderpath, directly across from them. "It's not interested in us," he hissed. "It's found some much easier prey." The lump of fluff looked like a young rabbit or perhaps a very fat vole.

"ThunderClan won't like having a fox stealing their fresh-kill," Archeye commented gleefully.

"That's not fresh-kill!" Hollyflower burst out. "That's a *kit*!" She sprang onto the Thunderpath before the other cats could stop her and raced across to stand over the tiny cat. "Get away!" she spat at the fox.

Archeye glanced sideways at Brackenfoot. "I suppose we'd better join in before she loses both her ears," he muttered.

Brackenfoot sighed. Yes, all kits had to be protected whichever Clan they came from, but this kit was still on its own territory! Couldn't they wait for a ThunderClan patrol to come to the rescue?

Clearly not. Hollyflower was advancing on the fox, putting herself between it and the kit. Protecting another Clan's kit was one thing; saving your denmate from being savaged was another.

Side by side, Brackenfoot and Archeye pelted across the hot black stone, screeching a battle cry. The fox jumped back and growled, baring long pointed fangs.

"You don't scare us!" Hollyflower yowled. She lashed out with her claws unsheathed and drew her paw back clogged with reddish hair. The fox snapped at her, its breath foul as crow-food.

Brackenfoot reared up onto his hind legs and swiped with both front paws, catching the fox on its ears. At the same time, Archeye ducked low and ran at its snout, striking as he shot past. The fox shook its head, scattering scarlet drops from its muzzle.

"Go, warriors, go!" squealed the ThunderClan kit. Brackenfoot had almost forgotten it was there. He aimed one more blow at the fox before dropping to all four paws and springing backward, out of range of the cracking jaws. The fox snarled once more, then turned tail and vanished into the undergrowth.

"Wow! You were great!" called the kit. "The way you sliced his nose! And swiped his ears! I wish I could fight like that!" the kit continued.

Brackenfoot padded forward. "What's your name?"

The kit gazed up at him with huge amber eyes. "Tigerkit," he mewed.

"Well, Tigerkit, one day you will be able to fight like us, if you listen to your mentor and train really hard. But you shouldn't even be out of your camp. What if we hadn't seen you? That fox would have made fresh-kill out of you!"

"But he didn't!" Tigerkit gloated, bouncing on his toes. "Because you saved me!"

Brackenfoot realized there was no talking sense to this mouse-brained tuft of fur. "Just be more careful from now on," he growled. Then, nodding to his Clanmates, he led them back across the Thunderpath.

The kit watched them go, stretching his neck to keep them in sight. "May StarClan walk your path!" he squeaked. "Thanks for rescuing me! ShadowClan will always be my friends! One day I'll help you, too!"

CODE THIRTEEN

THE WORD OF THE CLAN LEADER IS THE WARRIOR CODE.

Not every article of the warrior code is born out of wisdom, and it might seem that this one came from a dangerous lapse of judgment in all Clan leaders. Even so, this piece of code has survived unchallenged all these moons. Why? In reality, leaders take advice from their medicine cat and senior warriors—one cat alone rarely makes a decision. And the best warriors have never been afraid to challenge their leader, even at the risk of breaking the code. But come what may, the leader has to bear responsibility for what happens, and such a heavy burden deserves our respect. The code guarantees it.

Darkstar's Law

Raincloud held her breath as Darkstar heaved himself onto the Great Rock. The SkyClan leader was nearing the end of his ninth life and looked painfully frail as he scrabbled with his hind legs to boost himself up. Vinestar, the ThunderClan leader, came over and helped him by sinking his teeth into Darkstar's scruff and hauling him the last tail-length. Darkstar was too breathless to thank him, and lay on his side, panting, while the fifth leader, Yellowstar of ShadowClan, jumped up.

The SkyClan leader had been a strong and well-respected warrior for all his lives. Raincloud had been his deputy for many moons and dreaded the day she would have to watch him slip away from his Clan forever.

She stood with the other deputies at the base of the Great Rock and faced the cats who had come to the Gathering.

The RiverClan leader, Talonstar, began with a report of Twolegs staying in the fields on the far side of their territory; they came every greenleaf and didn't even seem to know the cats were there, but this time some of them had brought dogs, which had come dangerously close to the camp. Talonstar assured the other Clans that his warriors had chased them off with their tails between their legs.

Birchstar of WindClan announced a new litter of kits and two new warriors, then Yellowstar described an old, mangy fox that had been causing trouble on the edge of ShadowClan's territory because it didn't seem to be afraid of anything. Then Vinestar took his place on the edge of the rock.

"We have three new litters of kits and four new warriors," he announced with a flick of his long gray tail. "We thank StarClan for making the prey in ThunderClan run well this season, and we hope we can continue to feed ourselves in leaf-fall and leaf-bare."

He glanced sideways at Darkstar, whose head was hanging down with his eyes closed. Raincloud wondered if he had missed the thorn-sharp edge to Vinestar's report. ThunderClan patrols had been spotted more and more frequently on the boundary that they shared with SkyClan: not just border patrols, but hunting patrols, too. Raincloud suspected that, with so many new mouths to feed, they were starting to look beyond their territory for sources of fresh-kill.

Talonstar nudged Darkstar and the old tom's head jerked upright. Darkstar padded to the edge of the Great Rock. His milky yellow eyes gazed down at the cats in the hollow.

"Cats of all Clans," Darkstar began in a voice as thin as a whisker; the cats in the hollow fell silent, and Raincloud relaxed. "I, too, have an announcement. I wish to give part of SkyClan's territory to ThunderClan, to feed their new kits."

Raincloud stared at her Clan leader in disbelief. All along the line of SkyClan cats, fur bristled and cats whispered to one another in alarm. Raincloud glanced at Twigtail, the medicine cat, who shook his head and looked as stunned as she felt.

Darkstar raised his head and, outlined in moonlight, it was suddenly possible to see him as the great warrior he had once been. "ThunderClan may have the stretch of territory on our border as far as the silver birch on the riverbank on one side and the yellow Twoleg nest on the other. May these hunting grounds be as good to them as they have been to us!"

Raincloud jumped to her feet. She couldn't listen in silence any longer. "Darkstar, are you sure?" she pleaded. She hated that all the other Clans would see her challenge her own leader, but she didn't know what else she could do. Darkstar was handing nearly a quarter of SkyClan to their neighbors! Was he so terrified of conflict that he wanted to make peace with Vinestar before the borders were threatened?

Raincloud felt all the eyes from the watching cats burn into her pelt. Ignoring the gasps of shock, she jumped onto the rock

CODE
13

and put her face close to Darkstar's. "What are you doing?" she hissed. "Don't you trust your warriors to defend our territory? No Clan has ever given away part of its hunting grounds before!"

Darkstar pulled away from her, his mouth set in a stubborn line. "ThunderClan has more mouths to feed than we do. SkyClan can always extend on its other boundaries."

"No, we can't!" Raincloud twitched her tail in exasperation. "Twoleg nests block us on one side and the treecutplace on the other. And the warrior code says that we must protect our borders at all times!"

Darkstar looked at her, and she was unnerved by the strength in his yellow gaze. He stood up, and the cats below fell silent as if they were waiting for the next lightning strike he would drop among them.

"Forgive my insolent deputy," he rasped. "She does not understand what it means to be truly loyal to her Clan. Vinestar, the land is yours. My warriors will set new border marks tomorrow."

Vinestar dipped his head. His eyes were narrowed and full of questions, but he didn't challenge the generous offer.

Raincloud looked desperately up at the sky. Was StarClan really going to let this happen? But the full moon floated on, a perfect shining disk. There wasn't a single cloud in the sky. Their warrior ancestors could not have made it clearer that Darkstar could do as he wished with the territory that belonged to his Clan.

Her tail drooping, Raincloud turned to leave the Great Rock. It would be up to her to send out patrols to change the boundaries and shrink SkyClan's hunting grounds.

"Wait!" Darkstar ordered. Raincloud stopped and looked around.

"I want you to be my witness to a new law for the warrior

code," the SkyClan leader rasped. His eyes were gleaming now but not quite focused. Raincloud felt her pelt stand on end. Had her leader gone mad, right in the middle of a Gathering?

"No other leader should have to face such insubordination in front of the other Clans," Darkstar announced. "I propose a law that the word of a leader is the warrior code. What we say must never be challenged. StarClan gave us the power to lead; StarClan would wish it to be so."

Oh, no. That can't be made part of the warrior code. Leaders are cats, first and foremost, good and bad or a mixture of both. Raincloud realized her mouth had dropped open and she was shaking her head. She forced herself to stay still, and closed her mouth in case she said something that made Darkstar even angrier. She didn't care about being punished herself, but it suddenly felt as if she was all her Clan had left.

"I support the new law!" Vinestar declared.

CODE
13

There's a surprise. Raincloud waited for one of the leaders to point out how ridiculous this was, that there was more than one cat in each Clan with a worthwhile opinion, but the other three cats stepped forward in turn to agree with Vinestar. Yellowstar's eyes were troubled, and Talonstar's deputy stared hard at the RiverClan leader as if challenging the wisdom of his decision, but the law was accepted. The word of a Clan leader was now to be treated as if it was part of the warrior code.

As if sensing that several cats in the hollow were about to protest, Vinestar quickly announced that the Gathering was over and leaped down from the Great Rock. His Clanmates swarmed around him as he led them up the slope and out of the hollow. The other leaders followed, leaving Darkstar to dismount last of all, his stiff joints creaking. He paused as he went past Raincloud, who was still sitting in the shadows at the edge of the rock.

"You may continue to serve as my deputy," he croaked. "But never challenge me like that again. The borders will change at dawn."

He sprang down to the ground and beckoned the SkyClan cats with his tail. They headed out of the hollow, still muttering to one another. One or two glanced anxiously back at Raincloud, as if they thought she might have been exiled for arguing with Darkstar at the Gathering. *No. Just humiliated.* But Raincloud knew she wouldn't leave. SkyClan deserved better than that. Better than Darkstar, even.

She stayed on the rock until the shadows had stopped rustling with departing cats. She stared up at the moon, still expressionless and cloud-free. *Did you really want this, StarClan?* she wailed silently. *What happens when a leader comes who wants to change everything? Turn the Clans against one another, wipe out all the values we have ever lived by?*

What will you do then?

An Empty Prayer:
Gloudstar Speaks

Few cats know of the fifth Clan that once lived in the forest.
SkyClan cats were the highest jumpers and lived among the tall trees
where they snatched birds from the branches. But long ago, SkyClan
was driven out of its territory by Twoleg monsters, and then driven
out of the forest by the remaining four Clans, erased from Clan
memory by a legacy of guilt. Come with me, to SkyClan in its new
territory, under new skies, far from the forest.

The gorge is so quiet when night falls. It makes my Clan uneasy; they are used to hearing the rustle of branches and the call of birds above them—not just endless sky splashed with stars, more than I ever imagined there would be when we lived in the forest. I wonder if any of our warrior ancestors can see us. And if they could, would they listen? I know those cold fragments of light in the sky are not my warrior ancestors. StarClan stopped watching over us long ago, as soon as the Twolegs attacked our territory with tree-eating monsters, churning up the ground to build their nests of hard red stone.

My poor Clan. Was I right to bring them here, so far from their home? Perhaps we should have fought to stay in the forest, mustered the last remains of our strength to take on ThunderClan or WindClan and steal some of their territory. Not ShadowClan or RiverClan, though: We would never have developed a taste for frogs or fish, however hungry we were.

CODE
13

We traveled far to come here, and I want this to be a home to us as much as the forest was for all those countless moons. We have caves for shelter, fresh water to drink, and there's prey enough if we are patient and learn to stalk in the open rather than through branches high above the ground. Yesterday Buzzardtail and Mousefang brought back a squirrel, so there must be trees close by. Maybe tomorrow I will explore beyond the cliffs. I have to: My Clan should not know more about our new territory than I do.

But I am so tired. I ask only for a place to sleep that is sheltered from the wind and rain, and a mouthful of prey. Maybe not even that: Do I really want to live for moons in this strange place carved out of sand? Everything is different without Birdflight. When I sleep, my dreams are dark and empty, and whatever I eat tastes of nothing.

I brought my Clan to a place where I thought they could live, but it seems that isn't enough. These stars are as unfamiliar to them as they are to me, so I am their only link to the way we used to live. *The word of the Clan leader is the warrior code.* So they watch me and wait for me to tell them that everything will be all right, that SkyClan will rise once more to be strong and proud, rulers of their territory.

But this is not our territory. This is an empty gorge, a tunnel through orange rock with the sky for its roof. Our ancestors are no longer with us—if they ever were at all. Our fresh-kill pile used to whisper with the sound of plump, thick-feathered birds; now we eat mice and rabbits, when we are swift enough to catch them.

I hear my cats wailing like kits in the dead of night, wishing they could go back to the forest. But there is nothing left for us there. This is our home now. We will learn to catch prey and defend our borders against whatever other cats live near here. We do not need our warrior ancestors, or the other Clans, to tell us what to do. My cats trusted me enough to follow me here; I cannot let them down. Birdflight would never have wanted that.

As long as I am here, SkyClan will survive.

The word of the Clan leader *is* the warrior code.

CODE
13

CODE FOURTEEN

AN HONORABLE WARRIOR DOES NOT NEED TO KILL OTHER CATS TO WIN HIS OR HER BATTLES, UNLESS THEY ARE OUTSIDE THE WARRIOR CODE OR IT IS NECESSARY FOR SELF-DEFENSE.

I know you kittypets think we are fierce, bloodthirsty creatures who line our nests with the fur of our enemies, but we are not. Battles with cats who do not live in Clans are far more likely to result in death, because those cats often have no sense of the honor in a victory without bloodshed. Now you are about to discover what bitter experience taught—that the way of the warrior does not have to be steeped in blood.

The Medicine Cats Decide

Mossheart finished chewing the marigold leaves to a pulp and spat them carefully onto a leaf. "These should help the infection," she told the mottled gray tom lying awkwardly on his side. The jagged cut smelled of crow-food and looked yellow around the edges, and the skin surrounding it was tender and inflamed.

"If I ever catch that mangy WindClan cat who did it, I'll rip out his throat," Smoketalon muttered through clenched teeth.

CODE TWELVE

Mossheart shook her head. "Then his Clan will lose a warrior and swear vengeance on ShadowClan, and it will go on forever. Back and forth, shedding blood on one side of the border or the other, until the stars grow old."

"We have to defend our boundaries!" Smoketalon hissed. "The warrior code says so."

Mossheart sighed. The border skirmishes between ShadowClan and its neighbor WindClan had grown more and more violent in recent moons, with warriors from both sides darting across the Thunderpath on raids. Neither Clan was short of food, and it wasn't as if WindClan had developed a taste for frogs or ShadowClan had gained the swiftness needed to catch rabbits. It was nothing but mouse-brained pride that made each Clan refuse to be the first to stop. A WindClan warrior had died last moon, and a ShadowClan she-cat had been lamed and would never be able to hunt or fight for her Clan again.

Mossheart finished packing the wound with juicy green pulp and laid cobwebs on top in an attempt to hold the edges of the cut together and keep the poultice in place. "Don't move until I tell you," she warned Smoketalon. She pushed some dry moss under his head to make him more comfortable, then padded out of her den to clear her head of the bitter marigold scent.

Several of her Clanmates were standing on the far side of the clearing, staring into the trees with their ears pricked. A white she-cat, her belly round with kits, turned to look at Mossheart. "They're fighting again," she meowed. "Listen."

Oh, StarClan, no!

Mossheart padded forward to stand beside Lilyfur. Mossheart's pelt felt strangely hot and sticky, and there was a sour scent in her nose. She looked down. Her dark tortoiseshell fur was drenched in scarlet blood that ran down her legs and dripped onto the ground.

CODE
14

Mossheart opened her mouth to cry out and choked on a thick, salty clot. Retching, she spat it out.

"Mossheart? Are you all right?"

Mossheart opened her eyes. Lilyfur was bending over her, and Mossheart's fur was healthy and clean.

"Have you got a furball stuck in your throat?"

"No. I . . ." Mossheart straightened up. The only taste in her mouth was marigold juice. Faint sounds of battle drifted on the breeze: yowls and thuds as cats hit the ground, the rip of claws through fur. *So much blood . . .*

Mossheart bolted toward the noise.

"Wait!" Lilyfur called. "Where are you going?"

"We have to stop the battle!" Mossheart screeched without slowing down. Her vision must have been a message from StarClan that the cats in the forest were in danger of drowning in bloodshed.

Paws thudded behind her, and she realized Lilyfur was following. "Go back!" she panted. "Your kits . . ."

"My kits will be fine," Lilyfur wheezed. "I've watched you enough times to be useful." She risked a glance sideways at Mossheart. "It's going to be bad, isn't it? I mean, worse than before."

Mossheart nodded.

The two cats burst out of the trees into a clear patch of ground not far from the Thunderpath. The air tasted of monsters and the bushes at the edge were black and shriveled from the creatures' foul breath. A tangle of bleeding, screeching cats wrestled in the center of the clearing. Mossheart narrowed her eyes. Two large patrols, from the look of it, each containing several apprentices as well as warriors.

"Stop!" came a screech from the far side of the clearing, and a

small gray face appeared from the blackened bushes. "Stop right now!" he yowled again.

"It's Swiftfoot!" Mossheart mewed, recognizing the WindClan medicine cat from Gatherings.

The gray tom stepped around the motionless body of one of his Clanmates with a rueful glance and marched up to the nearest tussle. "Enough!" he ordered. "There is nothing to be won here!"

The two cats paused and stared at him. They stepped back and Swiftfoot gave the WindClan warrior a shove with his nose. "Go home!" he hissed. To Mossheart's astonishment, the cat spun around and ran into the bushes that separated the clearing from the Thunderpath. The ShadowClan warrior, a dark brown tabby called Logfur, bunched his haunches, ready to leap back into battle, but Mossheart hurtled up to him and planted herself in her way.

"You heard what Swiftfoot said! Go home!"

"There's a battle to be fought," Logfur growled.

"Not anymore," Mossheart replied.

Logfur glared at her, then slunk away, leaving a thin trail of blood from a cut on his tail.

"What in the name of StarClan are you doing?" demanded a voice.

Mossheart spun around. Silvermask stood behind her, the gray stripe on his face stained with blood. "Do you want us to lose?" he growled.

"No. I want you to *live*," Mossheart spat. "Are you going to keep fighting until there are no warriors left at all?" She flicked her tail at the bodies that lay slumped on the ground. "Three more cats dead? How is this going to help?"

"Because two of them are WindClan, which means two fewer enemies for us." Silvermask curled his lip in triumph.

Mossheart shook her head. "You are more mouse-brained than I thought," she mewed sadly.

Behind them, the warriors were staggering apart, stumbling into the undergrowth in the direction of their own territories. Silvermask eyed them in disgust. "Are you happy now, Mossheart? We could have won that battle."

"No, you couldn't. Every battle is a loss."

With a hiss, the deputy limped away. Mossheart decided she'd wait a while before telling him his wounds needed to be treated with goldenrod. Lilyfur padded up. "Is there anything I can do to help?" she offered.

Mossheart gazed around the clearing. Two WindClan cats wouldn't be making their own way back to their camp, and neither would a ShadowClan apprentice, Spottedpaw. Mossheart gulped as she looked at his little brown body. A warm breeze stirred the fur on his flank, making it look as if he were breathing. But the scent of death hung over him, and his bright blue eyes were glazed and milky.

Swiftfoot glanced up at Mossheart. "I am sorry for your loss," he meowed.

"And I for yours," Mossheart replied dully.

"This has to stop!" Swiftfoot hissed, startling Mossheart. "If we lose any more warriors, our Clans will starve when leaf-bare comes. How can StarClan let this happen?"

"Have you been to the Moonstone to speak with them about it?" Mossheart asked.

"No. Have you?"

Mossheart shook her head.

"Then we should go. You and me, and all the other medicine cats. If we all show up, perhaps StarClan will be forced to listen."

Mossheart stared at him. She'd met the other medicine cats at Gatherings but never alone, without other Clanmates around them. "How can we tell them what we want to do?"

"I'll visit them. I'll go on my own so it's obvious I'm not a threat, and I'll bring them all to the moor. Meet us by the pointed stone next sunrise."

Mossheart knew that Swiftfoot was right. The medicine cats needed to unite. They had the power to heal their Clans—perhaps this meant they could stop battles before they started.

"I'll be there," she promised.

Swiftfoot popped his head around the corner of the gorse as Mossheart approached the pointed stone the next morning. "I thought you'd decided not to come," he greeted her.

Kinktail, the RiverClan medicine cat whose tail had been crushed by a monster when she was a tiny kit, appeared behind Swiftfoot. Her eyes were shining. "I can't believe we're doing this!" she breathed. "All five of us, going to share tongues with StarClan at the same time."

"Maybe we should have done it before," muttered Swiftfoot. "Come on, we have a long way to go before sunset."

He led them across the moor, padding confidently in the

CODE
14

blazing sun. Mossheart walked beside Quailfeather of SkyClan, not envying her long, thick coat. Kinktail followed with Prickleface, the ThunderClan medicine cat with a temper to match his name. Mossheart waited for him to make a sour remark about what they were doing, but they traveled mostly in silence, speaking only when they needed to stop and find water. Above them, the sky was tinged purple as the sun slid behind the ridge, and a crisp half-moon appeared. Mossheart gasped.

"It's red!"

The moon was washed with scarlet, darker around the edge. Mossheart had never seen it look like that before.

"It's the color of blood," Quailfeather pointed out quietly.

Perhaps StarClan is already waiting for us, Mossheart thought.

Prickleface took the lead as they entered Mothermouth and began the long, echoey walk into darkness. Suddenly the blackness up ahead faded and a watery pink light started to filter along the stone walls. Prickleface quickened his pace, and soon they were running along the tunnel and exploding into the chamber where the Moonstone stood. The crystal reflected the scarlet moon tonight, giving off a reddish gleam that shone in the cats' eyes.

Swiftfoot nodded to the Moonstone. "You know what to do," he told his companions. "We have to ask StarClan if there is a way to stop the fighting."

Mossheart lay down and pressed her muzzle against the base of the stone. It was ice-cold and she winced, but gradually it grew warm and she felt it begin to throb gently, as if she were curled against the belly of her mother. She was safe here, safe and loved. No blood would ever be shed in the Moonstone chamber. . . .

"ShadowClan! Attack!" Mossheart jumped as Silvermask yowled right next to her ear. She looked around and realized she was back in the clearing by the Thunderpath, surrounded by a ShadowClan patrol rushing to hurl themselves on WindClan cats running toward them. She was watching yesterday's battle from the very start.

"You can't stop them, you know."

Mossheart looked down. A small brown tom stood beside her, his brown coat flecked with ginger. "Spottedpaw! You're not fighting!"

The apprentice looked up at her. "How can I? I'm dead, remember?"

"But this is yesterday!" Mossheart protested.

"No it's not. It's *every* day," Spottedpaw mewed. "This battle, and battles like it, will happen over and over, for all the moons to come, and there's nothing you can do to change that. We fight to protect our territories, our kits, our reputation among the other Clans. It's what warriors do."

"But you died because of it!"

Spottedpaw looked sad. "Yes. I wish I hadn't. I wanted to be the best warrior ShadowClan had ever seen."

Mossheart touched her muzzle to his fluffy ear. "I'm sorry, little one," she murmured.

Spottedpaw was beginning to fade. "You can't stop the fighting," he repeated. "But maybe you can stop the dying. That WindClan warrior didn't need to kill me. I knew I was beaten. If he'd let go of me, I'd have run away. He didn't have to keep biting me, harder and harder. . . . "

His blue eyes glowed for a moment after his body vanished, then they went out like setting suns. Mossheart closed her eyes as grief swept over her. What a bitter, bitter waste.

When she opened her eyes, she was back in the chamber, lying by the Moonstone. Her body was cold and cramped, so she stood up and stretched each leg in turn, arching her back and kinking her tail right over her ears.

"Well?" prompted Swiftfoot, who was sitting in the shadows with the other medicine cats. With a shock, Mossheart realized she was the last to wake up.

"I . . . I dreamed of Spottedpaw, the ShadowClan apprentice who died yesterday," she began. She stopped when she saw the other cats nodding to one another.

"We all dreamed of fallen Clanmates," meowed Quailfeather. "Each one said the same: that we could never stop battles from happening, but that they knew they had lost their fight before they were killed. They didn't have to die for the other cat to win."

"Victory without death," murmured Prickleface. "Do you think the Clans would accept it?"

"They have to," meowed Swiftfoot. "StarClan has told us all the same thing: that a warrior does not have to kill to be victorious."

"What if he is fighting for his life?" put in Kinktail, looking worried. "Against a fox or a rogue?"

Swiftfoot nodded. "There will be exceptions," Swiftfoot determined, "because some battles can only end in death. But for Clans fighting Clans, killing is not the answer."

"When should we tell our leaders about this?" Mossheart asked.

"Why don't we wait until the next Gathering?" Quailfeather suggested. "It's only a quarter-moon away. We can tell them about our dreams and suggest a new law for the warrior code. The leaders can't disagree with all five of us."

"That's right," Swiftfoot meowed. "And from now on, I think we should meet every half-moon to share tongues with StarClan together. None of us wants to see our Clanmates die, and all of us would be happy never to treat a battle wound again. Perhaps boundaries don't exist for medicine cats the way they do for our Clanmates. We should work together whenever we can, to preserve the peace and health of all the Clans."

He led them back into the tunnel that led to the ridge and fresh air and starlight. When they emerged, the moon had cleared and shone as white as ever. The cats began to head down the slope, their paws whispering over the short grass. Mossheart was convinced she could hear another set of paws close by, even though she wasn't near any of the other cats. Then she caught a trace of scent and knew who was running beside her.

Thank you, Spottedpaw whispered. *Your law will save the lives of many, many cats. StarClan will honor all of you forever.*

CODE
14

CODE FIFTEEN

A WARRIOR REJECTS THE SOFT LIFE OF A KITTYPET.

The life of the Clans is as far from the life of a kittypet as you could imagine. We hunt for our food, choose our own boundaries and fight to defend them, and raise our kits to follow traditions laid down by cats long since faded from our memories. Many Clan cats would say this makes us better than you; I would not necessarily claim that. There are good and bad cats everywhere—and good and bad within every cat. If every Clan cat was pure of heart and unfailingly loyal, we wouldn't need the warrior code at all.

Pinestar's Secret

"Hey, Lionpaw! Have you seen Pinestar?"

Lionpaw looked up from grooming his pelt. "I thought Pinestar went out with a hunting patrol," he told his mentor.

Sunfall narrowed his eyes. "I thought so, too, but the hunting patrol's just come back and Pinestar's not with them."

Lionpaw gave up on his tufty fur and padded over to the bright orange warrior. "Would you like me to look for him?" he offered.

Sunfall shook his head. "I want you to come with me on a patrol to check the border along the river," he explained. "The dawn patrol picked up some RiverClan scents as far in as the trees."

Lionpaw felt the hair along his spine bristle. Those mangy RiverClan cats! Why couldn't they stick to their own territory?

But when they went on patrol they found only the faintest hint of RiverClan scent under the trees, which could have been blown there by the wind, so they left their neighbors alone. When they returned to the camp, Pinestar was back. He greeted his deputy as soon as the patrol pushed its way through the gorse tunnel.

"Sunfall, is all quiet on the borders?"

"Yes," Sunfall replied. "Did the prey run well for you?"

Pinestar nodded. "StarClan was good to me."

Lionpaw was surprised. Pinestar didn't smell of fresh-kill, just flowers and crushed grass. Sunfall had told him he'd done well on the patrol today; Lionpaw hoped Pinestar would invite him on a patrol soon so he could show the leader how much he had learned. But Pinestar rarely went out with other cats; he preferred to patrol alone, he said, so he could hear and scent more clearly. Lionpaw was very frustrated. How would Pinestar know the best warrior name for him if he never saw him hunt or fight? He would only be an apprentice for two more moons, so there wasn't much time.

Lionpaw woke early the following morning, before any of his denmates. Outside the den, the air was clear and cold, with a hint of mustiness that suggested leaf-fall was on its way. The clearing was empty but the gorse tunnel was quivering as if a cat had just gone through. Lionpaw pushed his way in, wondering if whoever it was would like some company.

A reddish brown shape was just reaching the top of the ravine. Pinestar! Perhaps this was Lionpaw's chance to show off some of his skills. He bounded up the rocks behind him, intending to call out when he reached the top, but by the time he got there, Pinestar

CODE
15

had vanished. Lionpaw looked around. A fern was bobbing more strongly than the breeze was blowing, and the ThunderClan leader's scent drifted just above the dewy grass. Lionpaw put his nose down and followed the trail. He decided to see how far he could track Pinestar without being spotted. That would be a great way to show how good he was at stalking!

Staying far enough back to be out of sight and treading as softly as he could, Lionpaw followed Pinestar across the territory, past the treecutplace, and into the thinner trees. It was harder to track through the pine trees without being seen; Lionpaw had to rush between fallen branches and sparse clumps of bracken, hoping Pinestar didn't look back. He was so busy concentrating on not stepping on any crackly twigs that he didn't realize where he was until he looked over the bracken and saw Twoleg fences in front of him. They were right at the edge of the forest! But where was Pinestar? Lionpaw stretched his neck out from his hiding place and sniffed. The trail was still there—and it led straight out of the forest.

Had Pinestar chased a kittypet out of ThunderClan's territory? Lionpaw was sure he would have heard something like that. He crept through the long grass that grew under the outermost trees and sniffed the bottom of a wooden Twoleg fence. Pinestar had definitely climbed up here—there were scratchmarks on the wood. It looked as if this was a regular climbing place.

Lionpaw clawed his way up the wooden fence and looked down into the little square of Twoleg territory. Short green grass was edged with strong-smelling flowers, and a strange, leafless tree stood in the center holding bright-colored Twoleg pelts. Just past the leafless tree, the grass turned into flat white stone, where two spindly wooden objects stood on skinny legs. They each had a flat ledge at the top of the legs, and on one of the ledges a red-brown shape was curled, with a tail hanging over the edge. Lionpaw nearly fell off the fence.

What was Pinestar doing in the Twoleg territory?

Lionpaw was about to jump down and call to him when a flap in the Twoleg nest swung open and a Twoleg appeared. Lionpaw ducked behind some flowers, trying not to sneeze as the pollen tickled his nose. The Twoleg made some noises, and to Lionpaw's astonishment, Pinestar replied.

"Oh, thank you, I love it when you rub my ears! Could you do my back as well? That's perfect!"

Lionpaw peered around a leaf. The Twoleg was bent over the spindly object, stroking Pinestar's fur with one pink, hairless paw. If Pinestar hadn't been purring, Lionpaw would have thought he was being attacked. But he was *enjoying* it.

Pinestar rolled onto his back so that his hind legs dangled over the edge of the ledge. His head tipped back and Lionpaw caught a glimpse of his eyes, closed in delight. Suddenly afraid of being seen, Lionpaw scrambled back over the fence and dived into the long grass. He wanted to run all the way back to the camp and forget what he had seen, but he knew he couldn't do that. He had to ask Pinestar what he was doing.

"Lionpaw! What are you doing here?"

Pinestar was standing on top of the fence, looking down at him.

"I . . . er . . ." Lionpaw stammered.

Pinestar sprang down and looked closely at him. "Did you follow me?"

"Yes," Lionpaw admitted. "I wanted to show you my stalking skills."

"Well, I didn't notice you, so they must be good! Now, I expect you're wondering what I was doing with that Twoleg."

Lionpaw nodded. Every hair on his pelt seemed to be on fire.

Pinestar began walking back into the trees, and Lionpaw trotted to catch up. "The kittypet that lives there has been causing trouble for the last moon," Pinestar explained. "Straying into the forest, scaring our prey—not that he catches any, of course. But I decided to see how he liked it when I went onto his territory—and I wanted to give him a warning to stay away for good."

Lionpaw felt a little knot inside his belly relax. He had guessed this was the reason Pinestar had gone over the fence!

"He wasn't there, just my luck," Pinestar went on. "Then I heard the Twoleg coming, so I jumped on that ledge and pretended to be another kittypet so she didn't get suspicious. It was hard work, I can tell you!"

Lionpaw nodded. His leader was so brave and clever! Lionpaw would never have thought of pretending to be a kittypet!

"You won't say anything to the others, will you?" Pinestar checked. "I don't want any other warriors trying this. It's far too dangerous."

Lionpaw shook his head. "Oh, no. I won't say a word," he promised. His tail bristled with excitement. Pinestar must trust him as much as a warrior! Maybe his name would be Liontrust, or Lionloyal, because of the great secret they shared.

"I knew it!" Sunfall hissed. Keeping low so that his orange pelt was hidden by ferns, he looked back at Lionpaw. "Go back to the camp and tell Pinestar we're being invaded! Those RiverClan warriors have deliberately crossed the border. We can't let them get away with it. Pinestar needs to send a fighting patrol here at once."

Lionpaw nodded and whipped around. He squeezed past Bluefur and Tawnyspots and pelted back along the trail that led to the ravine. He jumped down the rocks in one giant leap and burst through the tunnel. "RiverClan is attacking us!" he yowled.

Several heads appeared around the clearing. "Where's Pinestar?" Lionpaw panted. "He needs to send a warrior patrol."

"I thought he was with you," meowed Thrushpelt. "I'll take the patrol to Sunningrocks; you go find Pinestar and tell him what's going on."

Lionpaw spun around and raced out of the camp. He could guess where Pinestar was: defending their territory against that pesky kittypet! Well, he'd have to focus on RiverClan right now, before those fish-faces took over all of ThunderClan. Lionpaw ran through the pine trees and threw himself at the wooden fence. He slithered down the other side, unable to stop on the top, and landed in a heap among the flowers. Shaking earth off his fur, he looked out.

Pinestar was standing on the white stone, eating a pile of brown pellets. The Twoleg was standing over him, showing its teeth and making soft, friendly noises. Pinestar swiped his tongue around his jaws and looked up at the Twoleg, curling his body around its hind legs. "That was delicious!" he meowed. "Is there any more?"

"Pinestar! What are you doing?"

The ThunderClan leader froze and looked straight at Lionpaw. A flash of horror appeared in his eyes; then he ran across the lawn. "You shouldn't be here!" he hissed. "What if that kittypet comes back?"

"RiverClan is invading!" Lionpaw told him. "You have to come!"

CODE
15

Pinestar looked down at his paws. "I can't."

"Why not? Did the kittypet hurt you?" Lionpaw peered at him but couldn't see any blood.

"There is no other kittypet," Pinestar mumbled. "Only me."

Lionpaw shook his head, confused. "You're just pretending to be a kittypet. So the Twoleg doesn't chase you away."

Pinestar glanced over his shoulder. The Twoleg was standing on the stone watching them. "She won't chase me away," he mewed. "She likes me."

Lionpaw stared at him in disbelief. "But you're our Clan leader! You can't be friends with Twolegs!"

"Then I can't be your leader anymore," Pinestar whispered. "I'm sorry, Lionpaw. I can't keep the Clan safe. I'm too old, too scared of losing any more battles. Sunfall will make a better leader than me. Tell ThunderClan that I am dead."

Lionpaw felt a surge of anger. "No! I will not lie for you! You might not want to be our leader anymore, but you could at least be brave enough to tell the Clan yourself. They deserve to know the truth, that you are leaving to become a *kittypet*."

He whirled around and scrabbled back over the fence. He heard Pinestar following, and the Twoleg call out in a high-pitched voice. "I'll come back, I promise!" Pinestar meowed from the top of the fence, before jumping down after Lionpaw.

They ran back through the forest. With a jolt, Lionpaw wondered what had happened by Sunningrocks. Had Thrushpelt's patrol been enough to drive out the RiverClan invaders? Would Pinestar be forced to fight for his Clan one last time? They reached the ravine and jumped down. The gorse tunnel was trembling as if several cats had just burst through it. The clearing was crowded with warriors and apprentices circling, some of them bleeding from scratches, others limping. Featherwhisker, the apprentice medicine cat, was chasing Rosepaw around with a mouthful of marigold leaves.

"If you just keep still long enough for me to put these on your cut," the medicine cat puffed, his voice muffled through the herbs, "I'll be able to treat the other cats."

"Treat them first!" Rosepaw protested. "That stuff stings!"

The cats fell silent one by one as they spotted Pinestar. When they were all quiet, Sunfall stepped out, bleeding from a torn ear.

"Where were you, Pinestar?" he asked.

Pinestar didn't answer at once. "Did you win?"

Sunfall nodded. "We chased those fish-faces back as far as the river. They still have Sunningrocks—that is a battle for another day—but they won't set foot across the border for a while."

"Good," Pinestar meowed. He padded across the clearing and jumped onto Highrock. "Let all cats old enough to catch their own prey gather to hear what I have to tell you!" he yowled.

Most of the Clan were in the clearing already, but they turned to face Highrock and settled down. Lionpaw joined Rosepaw and Bluefur, who was licking one of her claws. "I nearly tore it out on a RiverClan warrior!" she whispered proudly.

Lionpaw looked up at Pinestar. It felt so strange, knowing what he was going to say. The blood roared in his ears, and he didn't hear the start of the Clan leader's announcement, just the gasps of shock around him. Sunfall said something; then Pinestar spoke again.

"I have been honored to serve you for eight of my lives. My ninth will be spent as a kittypet, where I have no battles to fight, no lives depending on me for food and safety. Sunfall will lead you well, and StarClan will understand."

"The other Clans might not," Sunfall warned. "You won't be

able to come back to the forest, you know."

Pinestar let out an amused huff. "Oh, I can imagine the names they'll call me. I wouldn't be surprised if one of the leaders suggests an addition to the warrior code, that all true warriors scorn the easy life of a kittypet. But you'll make ThunderClan as strong as it ever was, Sunfall. My last act as leader is to entrust my Clan to you, and I do it confidently."

Sunfall dipped his head. "I am honored, Pinestar. I promise I will do my best."

Pinestar jumped down from Highrock and wove among his Clanmates for the last time.

A sleek black she-cat stepped forward. "Pinestar, what about our kits? Won't you stay to watch them grow up?" She nodded to the three tiny cats beside her. Two were weak and sickly-looking, slumped on the ground with glazed eyes, but the third, Tigerkit, was a sturdy dark brown tabby, who pounced on his father's tail. Pinestar gently pulled it away.

"They'll be fine with you, Leopardfoot. I'm not a father they could be proud of, but I will always be proud of them. Especially you,

little warrior," he added, bending down to touch his muzzle to the dark tabby's ears. Tigerkit gazed up at him with huge amber eyes and growled, showing thorn-sharp teeth.

"Be strong, my precious son," Pinestar murmured. "Serve your Clan well."

He straightened up and continued across the clearing. He paused once more beside Lionpaw. "Thank you," he meowed. "You were right. I had to tell my Clan myself. You have a good spirit, young one. When it is time for you to receive your warrior name, tell Sunfall I would have called you Lionheart."

He nodded, then padded softly into the gorse tunnel and disappeared. Lionpaw watched until the gorse stopped shaking.

May StarClan walk your path, always, he murmured to the old leader. *And may I be worthy of my warrior name.*

Lionheart.

A Change of Heart: Sandstorm Speaks

If Fireheart was just a kittypet, would he have gone to Tallstar behind Bluestar's back and arranged to stop the battle before it began? Would he have risked Bluestar's trust because he believed what he was doing was best for the Clan? Would so many of his Clanmates have supported him, even Whitestorm and Goldenflower?

Dustpelt tells me over and over that Fireheart can never be a true Clan warrior because he wasn't born in the forest. He belonged to Twolegs, who fed him that muck that looks like rabbit droppings, and made him wear a *collar*! He was such a show-off when he first came to ThunderClan. He always had to be best in training, or catch the most prey, and be the most solemn when we went to Gatherings. Dustpelt and I could never figure out why Graystripe was friends with him; he didn't seem to know what fun was.

And he was always causing trouble! Like taking Ravenpaw

CODE
15

away—Fireheart said he didn't know what happened when Ravenpaw vanished, but I saw them sneaking out of the camp. He always seemed to be doing something to annoy Tigerclaw. But now it looks as if he was right, and Tigerclaw was our biggest enemy all along. Would a kittypet have been able to figure that out? Not even Bluestar realized until Tigerclaw tried to kill her.

Maybe it's *because* Fireheart was a kittypet. He doesn't just accept the warrior code; he thinks about it and figures out how it's supposed to work. And when it doesn't, like when he should have obeyed his leader who ordered him to attack WindClan, he challenges it and does something different. Is that a weakness in Clan cats, that we do what we're told just because that's what our ancestors did?

Dustpelt insists that Fireheart doesn't belong in ThunderClan because the code says we have to reject kittypets. But we have to reject their *life*, not the cats themselves. And Fireheart has done that, hasn't he? He started out as a kittypet and chose to leave it all behind to join ThunderClan.

If I had to choose between Dustpelt and Fireheart to lead the Clan, who would I pick? Dustpelt is so loyal to the warrior code, he'd never dream of breaking it. The other Clans would respect him for that, which might make them more peaceful toward us. Fireheart would argue with any cat, in ThunderClan or outside, if he didn't think they were doing the right thing. I don't want to live in a Clan that is always at war.

But Fireheart won't fight a battle that he doesn't believe in. That's why he talked to Tallstar, persuaded him not to let his warriors fight when Bluestar led the attack on his border. Which means Tallstar must respect Fireheart and trust him, because he's always been friendly with Bluestar before now.

Maybe a kittypet can know us better than we know ourselves. Maybe it takes an outsider looking in to see the truth—like Fireheart knew the truth about Tigerclaw. I wonder if he'll ever see the truth in my own heart: that, whatever Dustpelt says, however much Fireheart breaks the warrior code, I love him more than I could imagine loving any other cat.

And if Fireheart knew, would he love me, too?

CODE
15

Rules That Did Not Become
Part of the Code: Leafpool Speaks

Not every rule that was suggested was accepted by all the Clans—and it was always understood, without having to be made part of the code, that every Clan had to agree.

Did you know it was once suggested that only cats of pure forest blood could be Clan members? Kittypets, rogues, and loners would be barred from Clan life—and those already living in the Clans would be expected to leave. I can tell you assume it was a ShadowClan leader that put this forward, but actually it was Featherstar of WindClan. After a hard leaf-bare, when only the swiftest warriors could catch any of the fleet-footed prey on the moor, she blamed her Clan's hunger on those cats who hadn't been born with the ability to run rabbit-fast. She saw the other Clans struggling to catch enough fresh-kill and was convinced that only Clanborn cats could look after themselves and their Clanmates.

Owlstar of ThunderClan argued most strongly against her—it was rumored afterward that he had kittypets among his ancestors, but he didn't. He just saw that all the Clans would be weakened if they had to purge their members of non-forestborn cats. Loyalty to Clanmates has always lain at the core of the warrior code, and what Featherstar was proposing would let Clanmates turn on one another and claim superiority for something they had no control over. As long as cats were loyal to their Clan, Owlstar insisted, then they deserved to stay.

Not long after that, Hawkstar's successor, Robinstar, put forward that Clans should eat only the prey they were most suited to hunting: fish for RiverClan, birds for SkyClan, rabbits for WindClan, and so on. This was shouted down by all the Clans. It was unlikely that all the birds in SkyClan's hunting grounds would ever get sick and die, even during the coldest leaf-bare, but fish, rabbits, and ThunderClan's squirrels had all been known to suffer from an illness that either spread to cats or reduced the numbers of prey drastically. Besides, every Clan welcomes a chance to taste a different kind of fresh-kill when it strays into their territory—though RiverClan are welcome to keep all their slimy fish!

It was Dovestar of RiverClan who wanted to make it law that every Clan cat had to acknowledge that StarClan controlled Clan life; to deny the existence and power of the warrior ancestors would be to break the code. Does it surprise you that this is not one of our laws?

Being a Clan cat is not about being forced to believe something. We are allowed to think for ourselves, you know! It is not law that you have to stay in a Clan—cats may leave any time they wish if they no longer feel true to the warrior code or loyal to their Clanmates. As long as we believe in StarClan and the influence it has over our lives, accepting the warrior code is easy and loyalty comes as natural as breathing. You cannot force a cat to be faithful. That would be far worse than letting them be honest enough to choose a different path through life.

EPILOGUE

You've now heard the history of the warrior code. Stretch your legs; you've been sitting a long time. I'll walk with you to the edge of our territory. I could use some fresh air.

Thank you for listening. Perhaps you understand our way of life a little better now. As you've heard, we're not always perfect, but we have a great deal of faith in our warrior ancestors. The code lives in us in our heartbeat, the blood pulsing beneath our fur. When we die, the code carries on in our kits, and their kits, for all the moons to come. StarClan willing, the code of the Clans will live forever, until the forest and the lake have turned to dust and our hunting grounds are no more.

THE #1 NATIONAL BESTSELLING SERIES

OMEN OF THE STARS

WARRIORS

THE FOURTH APPRENTICE

ERIN HUNTER

KEEP WATCH FOR

OMEN OF THE STARS

WARRIORS

BOOK 1:
THE FOURTH APPRENTICE

Dovekit and Ivykit—kin of the great leader Firestar—are poised to become ThunderClan apprentices. Soon, one sister will have an ominous dream—and will begin to realize that she possesses mystical skills unmatched by any other cat.

In the midst of a cruel season that threatens the lives of all four warrior Clans, bonds will be forged, promises made, and three young cats will start to unravel the secrets that bind them together.

THE #1 NATIONAL BESTSELLING SERIES

WARRIORS

SUPER EDITION

·BLUESTAR'S PROPHECY

ERIN HUNTER

SEE HOW IT ALL BEGAN IN

SUPER EDITION

WARRIORS

BLUESTAR'S PROPHECY

Four Clans of wild cats have shared the forest for generations, but tensions are running high, and ThunderClan must assert its strength or risk falling prey to its power-hungry neighbors.

Into this time of uncertainty, a kit is born. A prophecy foretells that Bluekit will be as strong as fire, destined to blaze through the ranks of her Clan. But with this prophecy comes the foreshadowing of her destruction by the one enemy she cannot outrun.

As Bluekit gains power and eventually earns her leader name, Bluestar, she fights to protect her Clan. But secrets from the past threaten to surface—secrets that may destroy ThunderClan . . . and Bluestar.